GW00385453

010814

THE WINNER'S GRIP

RICK O'BRIEN
Author-Illustrator

A humorous adventure novel for able readers, aged 10 and above

First published September 2018

ISBN: 978-1-7180-1748-1

rickobrien.writer@gmail.com

To my wife Kari,
Lotte and Sam,
for listening so attentively
to my stories.

Contents

Dear Reader

Are all stories true once told?
Then, this is a true story.
Every word of it is true.
Well, mostly every word.
You can ask my dad.
OK*, some of it* is the truth.
Still don’t believe me?
You don’t give up, do you?
OK, I admit it. Less than a quarter of my story is true.
All right, I’ll come clean.
It’s *all* made up. Honest.
Kangaroos don’t exist. Every word of it is a lie.
None of it ever happened.

Well, have a read and see what you think.

Deni

1 My Swing has Swung

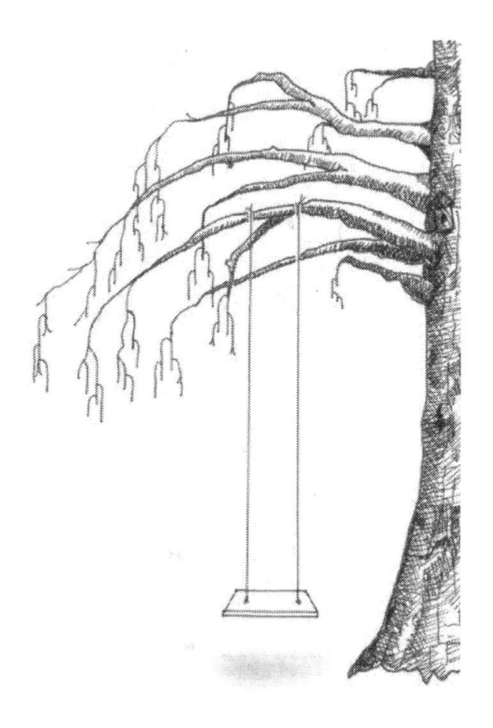

From the bottom of the garden, Dad cursed loudly. I wanted to see what he was up to so I skipped down the path. He wobbled at the top of a ladder propped up against our enormous silver birch tree and hacked with a knife at the ropes of my swing. 'I almost sliced my finger off, Deni.'

'What are you doing to my swing?'

'These ropes are cutting into the branch and strangling it. It's dangerous,' he shouted.

My childhood seemed to end with every swipe of his knife. I held back my tears. (I stopped crying when I was nine.) 'But you can't . . . I love that swing.'

The red plastic seat dropped to the ground. Like the legs of a dead dancer, its lifeless blue ropes, twisted and faded, stretched out on the grass. A crime had been committed and *he* was guilty. Today, something precious was lost.

I stared at the fallen swing and promised to myself that I would chop down his silver birch tree to pay him back. Dads can be so cruel.

'I get tangled in those ropes when I mow the lawn,' he said, stepping down from the ladder.

I'll miss my swing and the wind in my hair and that feeling of emptiness in my stomach when I'm pushed up into the sky. I came off it once and landed upside down in the conifers. Mum said I actually flew.

What was it with dads anyway? They just love 'jobs' around the house, most of which cost lots of money, never look that good, never last very long and never get finished. For as long as I could remember, my bedroom had only been half-painted.

'Deni,' Chloe called from the garden next door, her head just visible over the top of the fence. 'Are you ready yet? We'll miss the bus.'

In my Year 7 classroom, a handmade poster next to the whiteboard showed a boy with his eyes closed. A string of zeds flowed from his sleepy head. The caption read *Please do not fall asleep while I am talking*.

I hoped my class would stay awake today because I will be giving a talk about my trip to the rainforest of Brazil. I desperately wanted to tell everyone about the killer bees but the loss of my swing kept distracting my brain.

'Crazy Daisy,' my English teacher, told me, 'You're one of the best girl speakers in this year group, Deni. I bet you'll tell your story so well that the posters on the wall will rattle with excitement.'

Crazy Daisy sat with her legs tucked under her badly chipped, black table. Piles of open workbooks covered half the desk and the rest of the table was a home for pencil rubbers, a scattering of paper clips, elastic bands, a tea towel, pens and pencils, a shoe, various confiscated toys and a splay of yellow sticky reminders like fallen autumn leaves. She lived up to her reputation of being a bit crazy – a cup of tea ignored, having gone cold, stood on her desk with a red biro in it. A blue felt tip smudge ran across her right cheek and she had forgotten to put in her left earring. In my opinion, her green striped top did not match her blue dotted skirt. However, in spite of her quirkiness, she was a fantastic, A-star teacher.

I watched my classmates drag their chairs to make three wonky rows facing me at the front of the classroom. The boys clustered noisily on my left while the girls, and Danny Mulhouse, took the right. (Danny preferred to be with the girls, "because they laugh more.") A large gap between the two groups formed in the middle in case germs or the Black Death spread from one side to the other.

Standing in front of my twenty-eight classmates caused a rumble inside my stomach like a deflating football. I trembled slightly and tried to avoid eye contact with anyone except Chloe, who had plonked her chair almost on my toes. 'Good luck, Deni,' she said. 'You're gonna be great.' She made me smile and I almost forgot about my shrinking tummy.

Also in the front row sat nuisance Dirk Watchett. He pulled faces that reminded me of those scary creatures you see sticking out from the gutters of church roofs.

'Your story is all lies and rubbish. All made up,' he barked. 'You didn't go anywhere interesting. No one's gonna believe you.'

He expected some support from his little gang of mates clustered around him, but all he gained were a few snorts and a "Yeah, you tell her, Dirky." If his mates didn't show loyalty, they might get one of his playful wallops to the upper arm. He dished those out regularly along with Chinese burns, dead legging and knuckle thumping. He'd slap "kick me" notes on innocent backs, steal a younger kid's lunchtime chips or poke a pointy finger up someone's nose.

All very babyish for a Year 7.

I snapped back, 'What do you know, Watchett? My story *is* real and I *did* go to Brazil with my dad.'

Watchett picked on me at every opportunity, buzzing around my head like an annoying mosquito. Crazy Daisy said he liked me but had a weird way of showing it. Well, I didn't like him. I wanted to slap that mocking grin off his face but Miss would have marched me to the head's office, leaving Watchett pointing and laughing, enjoying every second of my misery.

I glanced in Miss's direction, waiting for a sign to begin my recount. She mouthed a silent 'Ok?' and raised her trimmed eyebrows. I nodded back.

'Dirk,' Miss called out. 'Try not to pull that funky-monkey face while Deni is giving her talk.'

Watchett immediately straightened himself and tried to sit still. Despite his off-putting face, winking eyes and sticking-out tongue, my moment of fame had arrived and I intended to make it a success. I glanced at my prompt cards, sucked in a deep breath and sneaked a peek at Chloe for good luck.

Then I told my story.

2 Killer Bees

Dad had a fascinating new job – finding amazing places for scenes in films. Brazil was his next destination and he said he would take me too. One of the world's most spectacular waterfalls awaited us.

I asked him, 'Why does this film, *The Zombie Queen, her dog and a three-legged dinosaur,* have such a long title?'

'It's what we call a *"working title."* Someone comes up with a proper name and we use that.'

There were nine actors with us (who moaned all the time), a film crew (who filmed the actors moaning all the time), and a group of strong local people who carried the cameras, food and things we needed (who never moaned). I moaned a bit and Dad moaned a lot.

‘I can’t believe we’re here, in the actual Amazon jungle. I thought this place only existed in books, but it’s real.’

It was nothing like the woods back home. For a start, my feet constantly entangled themselves in vines and creepers, tripping me up. And my clothes, dampened by sweat and rain, clung to me like a new skin. I felt uncomfortable.

‘I’d give anything for a large, cool cola with ice bursting out over the top of the glass.’

‘No cafes near here, Deni, I’m afraid,’ Dad said.

We had an expert to guide us through the forest. Fernandez Antonio Frederick Yakutsa was his name and he told me, ‘I is one-quarter eh Spanish, one-quarter Italiano, one-quarter Germany, and the rest Japan. I want be called Sid.’ He wore brown clothes and had a short beard and black eyes, “for seeing in the dark.” Sid’s skin tones exactly matched the colours of the jungle, but with extra dirt. He expertly led our group through the thick undergrowth, around the huge trees and down the narrow path that followed the river’s edge.

Occasionally, Sid shouted a creepy warning such as “poisonous snake” or “naughty spider,” which made me tremble and shiver all over until I had passed the danger zone. I never liked spiders. ‘Keepa your mouth closed in case spider jump inside.’

As we trekked along the jungle path, stories spread up and down the line of people about tourists bitten by the poisonous Brazilian wandering spider. Its bite caused horrible, pussy swellings. I heard about walkers lost in the jungle and died. Their skeletons, found years later, still had their watches ticking on their bony wrists.

I hated the clothes that Dad made me wear. They were far too heavy for walking in tropical heat. I wore a pair of untrendy, green army trousers, which would “keep blood-sucking leeches off your legs,” Dad said.

My ginormous boots would be more suited to a police officer. My green and brown army-type T-shirt, massively too large and ripped by spiky thorns, was plainly embarrassing. Hanging over my shoulder, a yellow water bottle with its wide plastic drinking straw became my essential friend. I constantly supped from it to relieve my permanent thirst. And guess what? No mobile phone – no signal.

Before we set off this morning, I sprinkled lemon sherbet inside Dad's ham sandwich. He usually liked my jokes. He took a bite. 'That cook needs lessons in how to make a tasty lunch,' he murmured, screwing up his sweaty face and spitting out mouthfuls of frothy, half-chewed mush.

As we ate lunch, the forest came alive with singing and whistling and monkey calls. I crouched at the base of a sixty-metre tree and, with my fingernails, picked dozens of wriggling minibeasts and flies out of my ham roll. More hovered nearby waiting to plunge into my margarine and vomit on my ham.

Sid joined us, sat down beside me and crinkled his nose at my festering lunch. 'Too many bugs,' I said. Dad remained nearby listening in, nibbling his lunch cautiously as if it might explode in his mouth.

A red and black beetle, the size of a finger, with pincers front and back, crept onto Sid's left boot. While I studied the creepy-crawly, Sid told me something he said I would not want to hear.

'There is killer bees in the forest, Dennis. Like me, they is a mixture from different parents – half African, half Brazilian. Very vicious and aggressive.'

'What do you mean, vicious and aggressive?' I asked. The beetle on his boot twitched and snapped its sharp pincers.

‘They is more violent than our local bees. They chases peoples when they gets angry.’

The beetle crawled up Sid’s boot and dropped down inside it.

‘What makes them angry?’ I asked.

Sid scratched his head through thick black hair. ‘They created a monster bee, sixty years ago – a scientific experiment went very wrong. The monster bees escaped from the factory . . .’

I interrupted, ‘You mean laboratory.’

‘Yes, lab-or-a-tory. They is angry bees because scientists tried to make them produce lots more honey. Now, bees spend all time trying to sting people. Some people have dead.’

Dad nibbled away at his lunch. His face squirmed as he bravely took yet another bite of fizzy ham. He seemed uninterested in Sid’s warnings about the killer bees.

Sid waggled his leg. ‘I will tell you if I see killer bees. I don’t want you to be frightened.’

But how could I not be concerned and frightened now he’d warned me?

‘You not worry, Dennis.’

‘I am *not* Dennis. That’s a boy’s name. I’m Deni. Deni Tutting.’

‘Sorry, Dennis Trumping. I not speaks best the English names.’

‘That’s OK, Sandra.’

With a loud yelp, Sid jumped up and slapped his left boot. He pulled the boot off and tipped the armour-plated beetle into a bush.

‘Don’t shout, Sid. You’ll wake the killer bees.’

Hunger drove me back to my lunch. I snapped at the edge of my ham roll and sucked up a mouthful of water through my plastic straw. However, I soon lost my appetite and stopped eating. Sid’s warning left me thinking only about bees. I threw the remainder of the roll into the river. It landed with a splash and a large fish snapped it up in one gulp.

'Tell me more about the bees, please,' I said to Sid. 'What should I do if I see them coming? Is there any escape?'

'I have plan of actions,' he said, sitting down on a fallen tree trunk and pulling on his boot. 'Killer bees fly closely together in a swarm. If you sees the swarm of bees up in sky and it is high up, then gets you down to the ground. That makes sense, yes? If you sees the swarm low down, you do opposite – you gets high up. Easy eh?'

'How can I climb such wide tree trunks and get high up?' I asked, rubbing my hand on the smooth bark of the monster tree next to me.

'You must climb, or run. But remember – they can run faster than you!'

'You mean fly faster than me?'

'No, you can't fly. But they can run *and* fly.'

I began to fear the worst. Snakes – I could shield myself with my rucksack. Crocodiles – I could thump them in the eye. Scorpions – I could clobber with my boot. But killer bees? What could be worse? (flying elephants, human-sized tortoises, six-metre long millipedes.)

'And whatever you do, Dennis, do *not* jump into the water. Them blasted bees will hang about until you come up for air, then they attack. They can smell your breath! They can hover above water for long times until you have to come out.' He raised a hand and wobbled it. 'Then they strike.' And he slapped his raised hand into the other with a loud crack. He noticed the terror on my face and added, 'But don't worries, Dennis. It won't happen. We checked with weather people before we leave hotel. They said it would be very today rainy. Killer bees hate rain so they stay indoors.'

'Well, it's not raining at the moment.'

'Right, let's move on,' Sid said, and everyone packed up their bits and pieces and formed a long line. We set off down the riverside trail towards our waterfall.

'I'm still hungry,' Dad murmured.

'Didn't you enjoy that scrummy lunch, Dad?'

'I'm not sure about this Brazilian food,' he replied, poking out his tongue. 'My lunch tasted fizzy. As soon as we get back to the hotel, I shall complain.'

Thirst rather than hunger occupied my mind. I took a short sip from my yellow bottle but the drink was warm. I imagined myself standing under that waterfall and having the coolest, most refreshing shower of a lifetime.

I felt a light tapping on my head, which suddenly grew heavier. A drumbeat played on the plants nearby as rain pounded us through the canopy of leaves. I stood out in the rain, face to the sky, mouth open, enjoying the shower on my tongue. I liked the feeling of the rain hitting my face. It relieved me of the annoyance of the nipping midges and the scraping of the sharp-edged grasses and leaves against my skin as I walked.

'Is that your first shower since Christmas?' Dad called out. But the sound of the rain shielded him from my answer as he just shrugged his shoulders and turned away.

The downpour stopped abruptly but I could still hear raindrops dripping off the tips of the leaves, however, the creatures were silent, which seemed odd in a jungle packed with animals.

There came a shout from further up the path – Sid's alarm – that phrase I did *not* want to hear today. 'Swarm ahead, Killer bees! Run for your lifes!' he yelled, along with further instructions in Portuguese or Spanish or Italian.

With all the panic that followed, I couldn't remember Sid's tips on how to avoid the bees. I couldn't even see the bees. Two of the strong men, no longer carrying their heavy bundles, ran past me at sixty miles an hour and shouted, 'Run Deni.' They disappeared into a clump of thick bushes. Should I follow them?

I heard Dad calling with urgency in his voice. 'Deni! Deni! Are you hiding? Are you OK? Put your rucksack over your head.'

I felt behind me and there was nothing on my back. Where had I left my rucksack? All I had on me was my water bottle and its yellow straw.

Very quickly, a spooky darkness blotted out the sun's rays, as though a wide umbrella had opened above me. I glanced up to find the cause but the branches and leaves of the canopy above, being so dense, got in the way. However, in the space above the wide river, where the trees from opposite banks had not quite met together, something did move, something dark and menacing. A cloud-like swarm of killer bees twisted and turned in its search for a victim.

Then I remembered Sid's tip. "If the swarm is high, go low. If the swarm is low, go high." Or did he say if it's high, go high? Low go low. I got all my highs and lows mixed up. So, I jumped into the river.

Not until I sank under the water did I remember Sid's other tip, "Never jump into water. They will wait for you forever." I was in deep trouble as well as in deep water. However, I found peace in that river, with its cool water running refreshingly over my whole, submerged body. I relaxed on that riverbed and gazed up through the clear water at the cloud of angry bees. They won't be stinging me. I felt safe and thought about my good fortune plunging into the river. But how could I continue breathing? If I floated to the surface, the bees would pounce on me for sure, as Sid had warned. I imagined their stings piercing and stabbing me through the useless thickness of my clothing.

I shook my arms and waved them about under the water, eyes wide open, hoping to scare the buzzers away. Then I froze with another thought – my flapping about might attract man-eating fish or crocodiles. I heard my own heart pounding and felt my lungs ready to explode, desperate for air.

I grabbed my drinking straw, stuffed it into my mouth and pointed it out of the water. I blew my stale breath up the tube then sucked in glorious fresh air. I felt alive again.

Keeping still and controlling my breathing, I relaxed just below the surface of the shallow water near the bank, watching all those killers hovering over me.

They must have thought; *she's had it when she comes up for air*. (Can bees think?) However, I had no intention of coming up for air. I had all the fresh air I needed down here – thanks to my plastic straw. I decided not to leave the safety of the river until every bee had moved away.

Sure enough, the swarm drifted off after a few minutes, except for one very angry bee that stayed and buzzed around the end of my straw.

Does yellow attract bees? Daffodils attract bees and they're yellow. One of our neighbours has a yellow car and bees always chase it. I should have bought a black water bottle.

The angry bee head-butted my straw, landed on the end of it and began to crawl down inside the straw towards my mouth. ("They can smell your breath!") My lips felt the thumping of its six legs as it crawled towards my throat. Its furry bottom was a tight fit inside the straw and it cut off my airflow – I had hardly any air in my lungs at all. I didn't want to leave the safety of the river in case there were other bees still roaming about.

I thought, *I'm* the Queen Bee round here – not you. My lungs were beginning to explode. They were desperate for air.

I pulled the straw from my lips, gulped a mouthful of murky river water, put the straw back into my mouth and blasted the water up the straw with my stale breath. And so I flushed the killer bee out and into the rippling river. I gulped fresh air again.

Then I noticed a shadow moving from the bank. Could it be the return of the swarm?

A powerful force grabbed my ankles and dragged me onto dry land.

'Deni, I thought you were drowning, but you seem to have discovered your own way of escaping the swarm.'

'Saved by a drinking straw.' I put it to my lips and blew air into his face.

'You're either very brave or very lucky, Deni.'

(Back in my classroom)
Miss Daisy smiled and clapped and the class joined in. I felt pleased with my presentation. If I ever have another story to tell, I will aim for an even larger audience because, when people listened to me I felt special.

Danny Mulhouse rolled up a sleeve of his sweatshirt and showed his arm. 'I got stung by a bee once, in Great Yarmouth.' A pencil sharpener bounced off his head.

'What an adventure our Deni's been on. And your recount was so clearly presented, interesting and exciting,' Miss said. 'Shame your father couldn't have been here.'

‘Yeah, cool,’ said Chloe. ‘I loved the bit when you jumped into the river.’

‘Deni, would you please pass round your souvenir straw so we can all see it?’

It quickly did the rounds, and when the straw came to Dirk Watchett, he folded his arms and refused to touch it. He became the grumpy boy who didn’t get the gift in *Pass the Parcel* at the Christmas party.

Danny Mulhouse winced, ‘I’m not touching that. It’s had a killer bee crawling in it. I got stung once.’

‘We know – in your arm,’ Chloe said.

‘No – in Great Yarmouth.’

3 Birthday Box Surprise

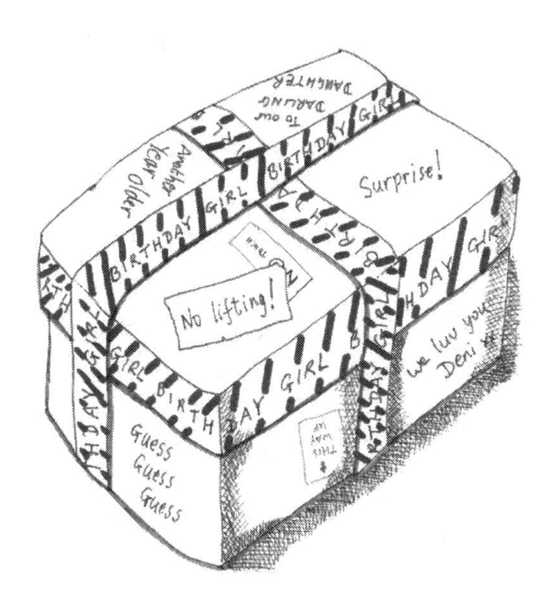

One week before my twelfth birthday, Mum and Dad decided the time had come for me to try my first coffee. A cup of nutty brown liquid appeared on the sitting room coffee table. It stank as though it had been strained through one of my dirty socks.

'It's cappuccino, Dad, not "capp-o-shi-no."'

He stopped stirring the froth round and round in his cup and said, 'I think that's how they say it in Italy.'

'Well, I don't think you should say "Capp-o-shi-no" here, Dad. You embarrass us whenever you order drinks. We get funny looks, don't we Mum?'

She said, ‘I *don’t* get funny looks because I always ask for a straightforward milky coffee.’ She yawned loudly.

I sat back and folded my arms. If they expected me to drink that stuff just to act grown up then I’d prefer to remain a child forever. I don’t force them to drink milk and peanut butter (one of my favourite refreshments).

‘Leave your coffee to cool a bit, Deni,’ said Mum. ‘Why don’t you go to the kitchen and see if your Birthday Box is ready?’

The very thought of that old Birthday Box made me dizzy. ‘Do I have to? It’s far too early for that frustrating game.’

With zero enthusiasm, I dragged my feet on the carpet and crossed the hall to the kitchen. My cardboard Birthday Box stood on the table, as I expected it would. Last night, I overheard them setting it up, giggling and whispering, shutting in their secret surprise with loads of childproof tape. Wasp-like, black and yellow BIRTHDAY GIRL tape sealed the whole box tight, locking the surprise gift inside like it was a prison. Just being near it gave me an instant tummy ache and a desperate desire to scream and smash plates.

My brain told me to make a tiny hole in the box and peek inside, but that would be too risky, too obvious. Mum read my mind and called out, ‘No touching!’

I scowled at the tatty box. Did it hold anything desirable? It had never done before. Since my eighth birthday, I’d suffered the same torture every year. Mum and Dad’s little game was for me to guess the “wonderful surprise” that lurked inside the box. Most children might enjoy such a challenge. Not me. I did not like surprises and I did not like guessing games. In four years, I’d only guessed the secret once, but I had a bit of help. I cheated. Cheating's OK as long as I'm the one doing it.

Mum had the receipt in her purse, so I took it. It was an indoor cricket set, suitable for ages 4+. That went straight into the bin, unopened.

Two strict rules gave me hardly any chance of guessing the surprise. *No lifting the box* and *no shaking the box.* However, nobody said I couldn't *listen* to the box. There could be something alive inside.

I pushed my hair to the back of my head and placed my best ear firmly to the nearest side. With a spare finger, I blocked my other ear. Anything inside that was living would surely make some sound. However, there were no longed-for noises of a cute little puppy scratching or yelping. And I loved dogs. I couldn't hear the ringing of a mobile phone and I had loads of friends to keep in touch with. And there was no purring kitten that might have felt my warmth through the cardboard. Nothing but pure silence. I supposed there might have been a fish in a bowl – they're quiet.

How could I ever see inside that box without x-ray vision? I'll just have to play their game again this year and make my three guesses. Maybe it's a stupid doll, or worse still, a jigsaw puzzle of a thatched country cottage with an old-fashioned family in front, with a horse and cart and ducks.

Would Mum or Dad have left the receipt lying about yet again? Where did they keep receipts anyway? Purse, coat pocket, bread bin, cutlery drawer. Maybe the rubbish bin would be a good place to start searching.

I yanked the bin out from under the sink and shook it madly, tipping its contents out onto the floor. Last night's tomatoey pasta leftovers spread across the tiles like slimy red slugs swimming in a stinking pond of dripping yoghurt pots, onion peelings, teabags, bacon rind and loads of bits of paper, torn packets, greasy tin foil and hoovered-up hair. It stank of sick, like the wheelie bin when it hadn't been emptied for two weeks.

I sat in my pyjamas and dressing gown in the midst of the trash, with my eyes half-closed, nose turned up and tongue almost out, picking through the waste with thumb and finger. I hoped and hoped for a piece of packaging or a till receipt or anything that would give me a clue. I liked winning.

I had just separated a soggy buttered crumpet from a badly scratched CD when Mum entered the kitchen still half-asleep, mouth wide open. She wore odd slippers and an inside-out dressing gown. Mum never worried much about her appearance – nor did anyone else. I thought her uncombed hair, cascading like a black waterfall over her stressed-out, puffy face, showed a less-caring mum this morning. 'What *is* going on, Deni?'

'I'm a little frog at the centre of a stinky pond.'

'It's much too early for games and mess. Such a shambles! I sent you to check out your Birthday Box, not to . . .'

Before it happened, I saw it in my mind – a foot slipping on cheesy sauce. Seconds later, she toppled like a giraffe on roller skates and faced me in the red, slimy mess. I felt her oven-hot breath on my eyelids, melting my skin.

'I saw a mouse,' I lied, remembering Mum's fear of small, furry mammals. She stood up and wrapped the inside-out dressing gown tightly around her legs. Sticky prune yoghurt dripped from her right sleeve. 'A mouse?' she asked, stroking the back of her head with a hand soaked in sardine oil. 'What sort of mouse?'

'You know! Small, a tail, four legs, tiny ears, a twitching nose, like . . . a mouse.'

‘I don’t think we’ve ever had a mouse in the house. What colour is it?’

‘Pink, I think. Yes. Definitely bluey-pink . . . with a hint of green.’

‘You sure about this?’ she asked, squinting down at me, pouting her lips and standing on tiptoe. She appeared a bit dazed and her bloodshot eyeballs slowly moved towards each other. Maybe she’d hit her head when she fell. ‘A bluey-pink-green mouse,’ she repeated. ‘I’d better call your dad. He’s a mouse-man for sure.’ She managed a brief chuckle.

‘Well, Mum, you’re lucky I’m here to challenge the furry beast face-to-face, head-to-head and sword-to-sword. I’m brave for my age, don’t you think?’

She turned and tiptoed through the rubbish as daintily as a ballet dancer. Stopping at the kitchen doorway, she put a hand to her mouth and called for Dad. He came striding at some speed into the kitchen, skidded on an onion skin and dived into the sprawling swamp of rubbish, chest first.

Covered in tomato sauce, each of us resembled supermarket ready meals from the Italian range. I stuck firmly to my mouse story while Dad stuck firmly to cold pasta.

I didn’t feel guilty telling a fib about the mouse. It’s a small untruth not intended to do any damage. After all, hadn’t they told me for years and years that a fat guy wearing red and white, and carrying a sack of toys the size of Fakenham, climbed down our chimney every Christmas and ate our food and drink? I once checked the truth behind that story. In 2012, I put food colouring inside Santa’s mince pie. Guess who had a blue tongue the next morning? Dad!

I reckoned Mum’s Santa lie was more of a proper lie than my mouse fib. But I had my punishment. I spent the rest of the day as Cinderella clearing up *my* mess. ("*You* did it. It's *your* mess. *You* get it cleared up.") In all that slime, I found no receipt. I'd wasted a day. And I'll never eat pasta again.

The Birthday Box took up too much of my thinking time during the following week. It sat in the kitchen peering over me like CCTV. I even thought it spoke – "You'll never guess in a million years what's inside me!"

I traipsed about the house not knowing what to do. Jobs, TV, homework and friends were ignored as though they didn't exist. I realised the game had to be played and that in the end the secret in the box would be revealed. Big deal.

I used some of the time annoying Mum and Dad – paying them back for keeping me hanging about waiting, waiting and waiting to unravel my surprise. I'd put spoons in the dishwasher mixed in with the knives or forks and not with the other spoons. Mum hated that. I blamed Dad. She shouted at him. They nearly started a fight. It's what they deserved.

A little garlic salt mixed into the sugar bowl found its way into Dad's coffee and made it taste sour, as though the milk had gone off. Dad drank it. He blamed Mum. She shouted even louder at him. They fought.

The evening before my birthday, supper finished and washing up done, we lounged about waiting for seven o'clock. That's when Dad turned on the TV. We sat on one long couch, me in the middle like a boiled egg in a sandwich. No-one talked until, rubbing his hands together and raising his bushy eyebrows, Dad nodded towards the Birthday Box, which had been placed on the coffee table, and said, 'OK Deni, we've got a spare five minutes. It's time to give us your three guesses. What surprise do you think we've got for you in the box this year?'

I rested my head on a fist. 'A horse.'

'I won't count that as a guess,' he said.

My brain wanted me to say, *a load of cheap rubbish.* But I said, 'Lip-gloss kit.'

'Nope,' he said, and beamed a *she'll never guess it* half-smile at Mum. 'Have another guess, sweetheart.'

My brain wanted me to say, *I don't care what's in the box. I'm not playing your silly game now or ever again.* But I said, 'A personalised neon bedroom door light and bell, please, batteries included.'

He delighted in telling me, 'You're nowhere near it, kiddo! One more guess and that's it.'

My brain almost forced me to say, *I shall make you two play this game on your birthdays in future and see if it drives you mad.* I said, 'It's that new cookbook *Recipes Your Parents Would NOT Like*.'

'No again! Sorry, kiddo. That's your three guesses used. Game over,' he said, appearing more delighted than he ever did whenever I tried my hardest to please him. 'Tomorrow, on your birthday, you can open the box. I bet you can't wait,' he said, pinching my cheek.

For one of their silly presents, I could wait until my *sixtieth* birthday – no problem.

When my birthday came, I wished the 10th of December could be fast-forwarded to better times. My dull twelfth birthday without friends, without cake and without candles, was too much of an embarrassment for me to have invited anyone. My best friend Chloe, ignored and uninvited, had neither spoken to me nor sat with me on the school bus for a whole miserable week. She wouldn't have eaten my birthday supper anyway. Dad intended to experiment with a special meal of tasteless egg salad with crushed cornflake sprinkles – in freezing December. He's totally useless at cooking yet he watches all the cookery programmes on TV; Hairy Bikers, Bake Off and MasterChef, but he learned nothing from them. I should get a court order banning him from cooking.

Mum covered the kitchen table with a fresh tablecloth and placed the Birthday Box on it. Dad nodded at me to open the box and passed some scissors. He and Mum stared at me so intently that my hands shook. I fumbled, entangling the scissors in the sticky tape. Ripping and hacking, twisting and pulling, I eventually freed the lid of the box and peeked inside – but saw nothing. I threw Dad a puzzled glance and almost threw the scissors too.

I turned to Mum, begging with tearful eyes for her help. She smiled back without offering the sympathy I craved from her. She seemed moody and offish, hardly speaking to me at all lately. Her once warming cuddles were fewer now and I missed them. Maybe she had decided twelve to be too old for kisses and cuddles. If that was the case, I didn't want to grow up. I felt lonely and cold.

'Don't give up so soon, Deni,' said Dad. 'It's quite a small object. Reach right into the corners.'

I plunged a hand into the box and crawled spider-like around the edges of its base. My fingers landed on something fiddly, small and cold. I grasped it and snatched it from its hiding place. I held it up and dangled it from my fingers. 'It's a thin gold chain . . . with half a medal attached.' My face slowly boiled and turned from Arctic white to volcanic red. Air raced into my lungs and stayed there for ages, puffing out my chest. My eyesight blurred. This medal thingy could never be what I wanted for my birthday, being neither expensive nor attractive. I just couldn't imagine wearing it. I hated it.

I looked closer at the thing as though it was dog muck. 'Isn't this my best costume medal, awarded in 2014 for dressing up as Hermione? You've cut it in half and put it on a chain.'

'Just for you, petal,' they said together.

'You can't steal someone's medal, cut it in half and give it back to them as a birthday present. How could you?' I looked at them in disgust, not certain which was pooier – medal or parents.

Dad said, 'Observe the fine detail.'

'What fine detail?' I sniffed the runniness from my nose and held the ridiculous object closer to my watering eyes. One side showed the top half of 2014 and the words 'best costume', and the other side had SAVE ME etched on it. I asked, 'Save Me! Save me from what?' And with a forceful Deni Tutting special huff, I threw the medal and chain across the room. 'Stupid present. I don't want it. I'm not playing this birthday game ever again!'

I stormed out of the kitchen and tramped up the stairs, forcefully stamping my feet twice on each step, getting louder and louder as I reached the top.

I collapsed onto my bed in a heap of bitter disappointment and cried my first real tears aged twelve. Where did all that anger come from? Could it just be my age? Or was it *me*?

I got up after a while and wandered over to the window to call Chloe (she lived next door). As I reached for the window handle there was a soft knock at my door. I turned, wiping my stinging eyes with my sleeve. In crept Dad with his head lowered, dangling the unwanted gift as though he intended to hypnotise me with it. 'Go away. I hate birthdays. I always get rubbish. Never stuff I really want.'

‘But this is no ordinary medal, Deni. Mum and I were told by a jeweller in the city that your medal would be suitable.’

‘Suitable for what?’

‘Suitable, he told us, to bring good luck – if I had it gold-plated.’

‘I don’t get it. Why is it in half then?’

I dropped onto my bed, folded my arms and pulled on my best bulldog face. ‘I’m going to look a right dork wearing that in public.’

He sat down gently at the side of the bed and pushed a tissue into my hand. ‘This half medal is the only one of its kind in the world. It’s properly called a talisman. One day someone special will turn up with the matching other half of this medal and that person will help you if you’re in danger. It’ll bring you loads of good luck.’

‘I don’t believe in good luck. I’ll make my own good luck if it’s needed. It’s bad luck I’m getting a lot of at the moment.’ I pushed myself up and sat. ‘And how will I find this special person anyway?’

‘They’ll find you. I shall give the matching other half to that special person – when I find him or her. You wear your half, they wear theirs. When you meet, join the two halves together to make one whole medal. It’s a bit of fun too.’

‘How can it be fun if I’m in danger?’

‘Hopefully, you’ll never be in danger, but if ever you are you can expect to be saved.’

‘You saved me from the Amazon river and I didn’t wear a lucky charm that time.’

‘That’s exactly what gave Mum and me the idea for this birthday gift. You need all the luck you can get in life. Promise me you’ll always wear it.’

‘So, if I jump off the tallest building, my hero will magically appear and catch me?’

'It doesn't work if you *deliberately* put yourself in danger. You've got to trust in the power of the talisman, and then it will work for you.'

I felt as though I'd been kicked out of my home and told to go it alone, at twelve-years-old, with just that ridiculous medal for protection against all the world's evils.

'Well, I don't believe in ghosts, vampires, zombies, tooth fairies, superheroes or your lucky talisman medal,' I said, and turned to face my Doctor Who poster.

Dad crept out, switching off my light on his way. 'Happy birthday, Deni,' he whispered.

Had I been too harsh in rejecting his rotten surprise? I mean, how many twelve-year-olds do you know who'd want a . . . taximan, or whatever it's called?

My body wanted sleep urgently but my dreamy brain put me on the edge of a red-flamed, erupting volcano. My feet felt the heat through my boots and I could smell burning rock. At any moment, I might topple over the edge into the volcano. And where was my special hero? Nowhere in sight.

What is a dream anyway? Just a random film in your head – a small TV in your brain. If you're lucky, you get to be in the film. But they never come true. When I woke the next morning, the golden half medal on its chain dangled around my neck. It gave me no feelings of good luck at all. Instead, I imagined my life would soon be in danger, heading down the slippery slope of doom, and that my birthday lucky charm would *never, ever* have the power to save me.

BEST COSTUME

4 The Rising Storm

I rubbed a clear circle in the wet on my bedroom window and watched the grey April clouds and the white lightning flash. Five seconds later, a forceful roar of thunder growled right above our house. I squeezed Garlic Breath, my teddy, a little tighter. 'Don't worry about that thunder and lightning GB. I'll protect you.'

Mum called from the kitchen, extra loud over a thunderclap. 'Deni! Do you want to look after Gran for a week or so?' I stuffed GB under my duvet.

Down the stairs I hurried as though my clothes were on fire. My feet flew over the last three steps and I landed in the kitchen with an enormous smile pushing up a pair of bright eyes. 'Did I hear you right, Mum? Stay at Gran's?'

She stopped washing wine glasses, turned and stared at me as though I had committed a crime. What had I done wrong now? Or did she have bad news about Gran? In any case, I quickly ditched the smile. 'Is Gran poorly again?'

'No, she's well enough. We've just been speaking on the phone about the weather forecast. We're in for some very heavy rain over Easter.'

‘I didn’t know rain could be *heavy*.’

She pointed at me as she spoke. ‘Stop being silly, Deni, or I’ll change my mind about you going.’

I faced away then turned back to stare at her feet and put on my worst sour face.

She continued, ‘You remember Gran’s house flooded a few years ago?’

I nodded a yes.

‘Well, we’re heading for a record high rainfall and your dad and I would like you to be with Gran as her house will probably be flooded again.’

‘Couldn’t Gran stay here?’

‘She refuses to leave her old house. You know how stubborn she can be. You’ve no school at the moment so it’s perfect timing.’

‘What use can a twelve-year-old be in a flood?’

‘You can be good company and help carry her stuff upstairs to keep it dry. She’ll be fine with you around and you’ll be fine with her. I think it’s fantastic that you two get along. You’re a credit to your family, Deni.’ She returned to her washing up.

Gran was great fun. She could be a bit forgetful at times. (“Where have I left my reading glasses?”) She muttered to herself, and she often went on and on and on about how desperately she wanted her kitchen worktops lowered (she has shrunk).

I joined Mum at the sink and blew away a cloud of soapy suds from her arm. She appeared pale and tired.

‘I do love Gran, a lot. Perhaps I should give her my birthday talisman for good luck.’

‘What? Oh, that thing. It’s not for *her*. Only *you* must wear it. Didn’t your dad explain all that?’

‘Mum, are you sure Gran’s OK?’

‘She’s fine, as I’ve said, and she’s looking forward to seeing you.’ Mum’s eyes filled with tears. She blinked and wiped them with a tea towel. 'She said you'll be smashing company in a storm.'

I focused closely on my mother's face. She's getting older. A shadow lurked below each eye. They reminded me of the neglected village ponds so common around Sumpton. 'You seem a bit . . . upset, Mum.'

'I'm fine, Deni. Just a bit worn out. I'm pleased you want to be with Gran and proud that you're mature enough to take on responsibilities. You're a decent girl.'

Encouraged by her unusually kind words, I smiled and clapped at the thought of staying at Gran's old farmhouse. It's where Dad grew up. He has taken me there many times.

After Grandpa Edward died, Gran got rid of the sheep, pot-bellied pigs and the hens that used to peck flying ants in the summer. I often shooed them out of the bedrooms. Her tumbledown sheds, abandoned chicken coops and disused pigsties became alien worlds where I'd search under old straw and cobwebby piles of wood for ancient tractor bits, rusty knives and farm tools. I kept my findings in a wood-wormy trunk, which I found covered in owl poo in the big barn.

Last summer, I discovered six rusty horseshoes in the old stable. I set up a throw-a-horseshoe game in the yard, which Gran loved. We played for ages until our arms fell off. It brought back memories of her childhood.

'Perhaps I could help Gran with the cooking,' I suggested, joining my hands together and pleading with a keyboard-like grin. Cooking meant I could nibble the tastiest ingredients. ("Keep whistling, sweetheart," Gran would say to stop me eating.)

'Cooking sounds useful. Now go and brush your hair, pack a few bits and pieces and Dad'll drive you there.'

I was almost back in the hallway when Mum called, 'Deni, come here kiddo.' She dried her hands on a towel and cupped them around my face. Her hands were still warm from the washing up. She brushed my cheeks with her thumbs. ‘You have the softest skin, Deni.’ I thought she’d start crying again. ‘When you were born you couldn’t stop smiling. You just wanted to start living right from that moment. And do you know what? You haven’t for one minute stopped wanting something special out of life. I hope you find it.’

For a second time, I was almost out of the kitchen door when she called out, ‘Deni – I love you.’

Parents can act a bit weird sometimes.

5 A Very Important Matter

Heavy rainfall, like a bath tap running on full, bashed its watery fists on Gran's roof as soon as we arrived. The car's windscreen wipers waved madly while Dad remained in the car. I got out, slammed the door behind me and dashed through the rain to Gran sheltering in her back porch. My feet and socks got drenched in seconds. Dad immediately drove away without one word to Gran – his own mum. He hooted as he passed through the outer gate. We waved, but I doubt if he could have seen us through the thick curtain of rain.

Gran appeared upset at Dad's speedy and unloving departure. 'He usually stays for cake.'

'He's been grouchy all morning – probably mad at me for something.'

We got straight to work stuffing rolled up towels against the bottom of doors. But water penetrates through the tiniest gap.

'How can it rain so much?' I asked.

'It's not just rain, sweetheart. I think the river's burst its banks.'

Her ground floor flooded first. That put an end to my cooking plan. By early afternoon, the cooker had half disappeared under filthy water, which sneaked into the house as silently as a prowling tiger. Sickly and slimy, it forced its way into Gran's little fridge, spoiling most of our food. I rescued a bottle of milk, some cheese and yoghurts. Holding the food in a basin above my head, I waded through cold water up to my waist and reached the stairs. 'Add those bits to our sweets and cake drawer in my bedroom. If the flood rises any higher we'll have to climb into the attic!'

'It's lucky you don't live in a bungalow, Gran. We'd already be in the attic by now.'

'I think you'd be better off sleeping in my room, Deni, next to me in the big double. You'll be warmer and we can store bits of furniture in your room. Now go and change into some dry clothes.'

Her cosy old-fashioned bedroom, with its wallpaper of red and yellow roses, gave me a warm feeling deep inside. I convinced myself that the roses had a real perfumed scent. That helped me forget about the floodwater pong. On the left of the bed, a monstrous brown wardrobe towered over me like an enormous skyscraper. I rummaged inside it and found a hand-knitted grey cardigan, about the size of Fakenham, which I put on. It almost reached the floor.

'You've turned into a granny!' she said.

What a cool gran! Seventy-one years old and she never complained – though I knew she had achy knees and could have moaned about them all day long.

There were no strict rules in her house and she allowed me to make up my own mind about things. She said I could eat whatever I wanted (biscuits and cake) and stay up until past ten o'clock.

Before bedtime, we sat at a round felt-covered table and fumbled through her albums of white-bordered photographs. Slowly, she turned the black cardboard pages, smiling as she remembered special people, special events and special days.

One large black and white photo, stuck on its own page, caught my attention. Names had been hurriedly scribbled over the picture. I could only read "Ringo." I asked, 'Who are those four guys with you?'

'They're The Beatles – a pop group. Grandpa Edward and my sister Sue took me to see them in London on my twenty-first birthday, lucky me. Edward arranged a visit to meet the lads backstage after the show. They made us laugh so much I cried. Dreams do come true.'

'We're they famous?'

'Oh yes, all over the world.'

'What makes someone famous?'

'Well poppet, you need to have people interested in what you do.'

'Do you think I could be famous, live in a castle, recognised everywhere, driven in a stretched limo, eat only ice cream?'

'Can you sing, poppet?'

'Like a bath being emptied.'

'Then, I'm afraid my answer is a no.'

I gawped at the five smiling faces peering out from the photo. A whole lifetime had passed by since that day when Gran and The Beatles were teenagers.

Waking me up from my daydreaming with a nudge, she said, 'You'll love this one,' and she removed a slightly faded picture from the page and handed it to me. A little kid in blue shorts, beaming a massive smile like a slice of melon, riding his red bicycle, perfectly positioned against a thick row of towering trees. A moment captured forever – Dad as a toddler learning to cycle. It's difficult thinking of adults as children. I tried imagining Mum as a child, but I couldn't get an image of her into my head.

Following a restless night's sleep, I got up, plodded across the soggy carpet to the top of the stairs, and stared down at the damage to Gran's home. Overnight the flood had arrived in force and the water level had crept up a few more steps. Bits of my Lego airport floated on the surface of the sludge, like confetti blown about at a wedding. The air stank, reminding me of clogged drains, soggy dogs and wet trainers. Every breath I took had the flavour of that water – the rusty bitterness of metal as though I'd been sucking coins or chewing keys.

Furthermore, the phone didn't work and the electricity had been cut off. Yet Gran insisted, 'I don't need rescuing. I'm staying put.' Mum may have been right when she said Gran could be stubborn.

Outside, treetops, hedge tops and telegraph poles stood out above the water's surface and were the last remaining signs of a normal landscape. Our country lanes and fields disappeared, swallowed up by a sea of destruction.

'Hey, Gran!' I called from our bedroom window. 'There's a dead sheep floating in the yard and its horns are tangled up in the snapped clothesline.' One of the horns stuck out above the water with a chirping robin perched on it.

'Guess what I found? – Edward's old radio,' Gran said, cradling it as though it was a baby. 'It still works. No batteries needed. You just wind it up.' She stood it on the felt-topped table, pulled up a couple of chairs and got the local news.

"The river Tann burst its banks yesterday, putting much of the Tann valley area under water. It will only get worse until the rain stops. Police are advising homeowners to stay at home until a rescue team arrives."

'What rescue team? I haven't seen one flashing blue light,' said Gran.

'You'd think your name would have been on a checklist of some kind and that boats, fire engines and helicopters would have surrounded the house and whisked us away to safety, making us famous like The Beatles.'

'I think we've been forgotten, petal,' and she giggled, blocking some of the sound with her fingers against her lips. She often giggled. (Dad called it chortling. "One of her many charms.") She giggled again as she stroked my hair with her hand. 'Poor little sweetheart,' she said, 'having to spend time with your old Gran, in a flood.'

'I don't mind. It's an adventure. But I miss sleeping in my own bed and I miss Mum and Dad, even though they upset me sometimes.'

Talking about rescue made me think of my talisman and I felt my neck to make sure I still wore it. My mysterious hero might appear and save me as Dad promised. Perhaps I should believe in good luck after all.

'Mum and Dad should have rescued us by now, shouldn't they?'

'Maybe they tried petal but were unable to get through all this water. It's so deep out there.'

'I'm not scared. Are you scared, Gran?'

'Not one bit. Tuttings are fighters, survivors. We can deal with a drop of rain.'

We played snap, apples and pears, and more snap. For lunch, we scoffed one packet of chocolate digestives, a slab of cheese with crackers, two Crunchies each, a can of fizzy and a tin of Frankfurters dipped in salsa sauce. We threw out the Scotch eggs because they were covered in maggots.

On our second flood night, Gran allowed me a special glance inside a decorated wooden box, the lid of which glistened with swirls and flowers formed by metal strips hammered into the wood. 'This box is very precious. Edward bought it for me at a Sunday market on our honeymoon.' She placed the box on her lap. 'Paris, nineteen sixty-two. Seems like yesterday. Anyway, the lady on the stall said a craftsman hand-made it in the snowy Pyrenees mountains.'

Heavy splodges of rain continued to pound our windows as we sat in the flickering light cast by candles mounted on dinner plates. 'Open the box, Gran, go on. What's inside?' I begged, clapping and shifting on my chair.

'Patience, sweetheart.'

It reminded me of my Birthday Box, but without being forced to do the guessing bit.

Her slightly shaking, wrinkly fingers carefully removed the lid, as though it were made from tissue. She took out a silver diamond necklace, a deep-orange butterfly broach and orange amber earrings, which she placed neatly on her table. 'I wore all these at my wedding, Deni. I felt so special. You should have seen me. Edward said I resembled the Queen.'

I tried the pieces on and I too looked like the Queen (a younger version of course).

By the next morning, the rain seemed to have eased and my worries about not being rescued increased. 'Gran, we must leave the old farmhouse before we're swallowed up and washed away by the swirling water – or worse still, the building crumbles.'

'This house is over four hundred years old. Its walls are made of plaster, not bricks like modern houses. It could collapse!'

'In that case, it's for the best that we leave now. We can look forward to a proper dry bed and a hot cup of tea.'

'Oh, I've missed my tea. But I'll miss my old home even more. I've been here all my life, Deni. I feel as if I'm abandoning the spirits of my dear family.' Her eyes sank as she glanced over to the bedside table at the framed portrait of her husband – a smiling, friendly gentleman in a striped suit. 'I've been flooded out before but this is the worst it's ever been (no giggle). It's like the river exploded.'

'It did explode – all around your farm. That's why we really must go.' And I put a hand on her shoulder and kissed her forehead. 'You can return once the water level's gone down.'

With both hands she touched her chin, letting out a soft sigh. Perhaps my idea to leave disturbed her more than I knew. But after a moment of deep thought, she seemed to perk up, smiled and said, 'I think you could be right, Deni. To remain in the house now would be simply crazy. What about my photos and things? I can't let the water gobble them up.'

'I'll pack them for you, Gran.'

On the bed, we gathered all her personal treasures – photos, jewellery and mementoes, and crammed them into an old, oval hatbox. She hauled herself on to a chair and placed the hatbox high up on top of her skyscraper wardrobe. I liked her idea of having a keepsake box. I'm going to start one of my own when all this flood business is over – and it's not going to be grubby like my wood-wormy box of rusty bits

'How are we going to get away, swim?' she asked, doggy paddling in the air.

'No swimming – we're going to row to freedom.'

'But there's no boat.'

I took her hand and led her to the bathroom. She pointed to her peach-coloured plastic bathtub. 'You don't mean? I'm not paddling about in that bloomin' thing.'

Under the bed, I found granddad's old toolbox, took out a wrench and undid both bath taps. At the last turn of the wrench on the cold tap, freezing water gushed out of the pipe, shot into my face and drenched the bathroom and landing.

Gran didn't seem flustered and said, 'A little extra water during a flood can't do much more harm.'

Firmly holding the facing side of the bath, we pulled and twisted until it came away from the wall. We dragged the bath out of the bathroom, laughing at our efforts, crashing into bannisters, denting walls and chipping paint off door frames. It wouldn't fit down the narrow stairs, so we pushed the bath across the top landing to the front bedroom. We opened the window as wide as it could go and hoisted the tub up on to the sill.

Gran held the bath steady while I blocked the plughole with the bath plug and walloped it firmly in place using a hammer. I loaded on board a hockey stick to use as a paddle, a bottle of fizzy and a packet of ginger biscuits for emergencies. Gran wanted to take her bedspread and matching pillows, a Wallace and Gromit alarm clock, an electric toothbrush, make-up bag and a small porcelain ornament of a boy wearing shorts. I said they would just get in the way.

An old pair of Gran's grey tights made a useful rope and I tied it through the hole at the end of the bath where the cold tap used to sit. Our bathtub now resembled a boat, ready to launch.

Gran held up an imaginary glass of wine and said, 'I name this ship Gran-Deni,' and we tossed the old tub out of the window. It landed in the water right way up and I held the toe end of the tights to stop it drifting away.

Using sheets tied end to end, with one end tied to a radiator and the other end dangling out of the bedroom window, Gran carefully slid down them. Like an acrobat, she launched herself off the sheets and into the old tub – which stayed afloat even with her shifting about in it.

I made sure she wore her slippers, for comfort. I swapped right for left, as a joke, and when she put them on she didn't notice they were on the wrong feet.

Down the sheets I slid, like a convict escaping over the prison wall, and squeezed into the front of the boat, hockey stick ready. I paddled like crazy but it seemed ages before we made any movement away from the house.

As we passed the big barn, we stumbled upon an unfortunate mooing cow stuck up a tree. She gawped at us as if to ask, 'Got room for one more?'

Gran nudged me in the back and giggled. 'I'm impressed with our boat. You're so clever, Deni Tutting – organising my rescue like this. I smiled back, loving the flattery she had given me.

'By the way, Deni, as soon as we're settled on dry land, I've something very important to tell you.'

I struggled to think what that could be and asked, 'Can't you tell me now?'

'Now's not the right time, sweetheart.'

'But I *want* to know.' I immediately felt ashamed that I had challenged Gran. Good job she couldn't see my reddening face.

'Then you'll just have to be patient, Deni.'

The 'very important' matter continued to occupy my thoughts as we splashed our way along a country lane, now a river, drifting from one hedgerow to another and occasionally crashing into branches and road signs showing just above the water (No Parking). We didn't know where we were, or where we were going.

We discovered that a bathtub does not act in water in the same way as a proper boat would. 'We don't have that bit underneath that keeps it going straight,' Gran said. 'That's why we often go round and round in circles like a bumper car without a steering wheel.'

With all our splashing about we were drenched, but kept our spirits up by singing and telling knock-knock jokes such as;

Knock, knock.

Who's there?

Doctor.

Doctor Who?

How did you know?

They might have been old jokes, but they made us laugh and made the boat wobble.

After about an hour paddling, the farmhouse could still be seen behind us in the distance. My arms felt as though they'd done a hundred press-ups, so I let them flop into the cooling water. Then, just as I thought I couldn't paddle any further, I spotted something and called to Gran, 'What's that up ahead?'

She peered around me to see. 'It's a little mound of earth standing above the water.'

'Land at last!' I shouted, banging the hockey stick on the side of the tub.

Gran screamed, 'Is it Holland?'

'Holland doesn't have hills. I think it could be the Isle of Wight.'

In our excitement, we drifted among some large stone ruins. 'I know this place,' Gran said. 'It's the old monastery graveyard.'

The tub hit a solid object below the surface and stopped dead with a jolt. My hockey stick had entangled itself in something. I tugged and wriggled, releasing it with a mighty jerk. As I raised the stick above our heads, parts of a mouldy brown skeleton slid down it and landed on me. 'Get it off!' I cried, ejecting myself and the old skeleton out of the tub and into the brown floodwater. I sank but Gran grabbed my wrist and hauled me from the sea of filth. I stood up and coughed.

'Hey! You're standing. The water's shallow.'

Once I had recovered my breath I said, 'We must be in about a metre of water now. I'll push you to the mound.'

With my last ounce of energy, I pushed and pushed, stumbled over a few rabbit holes, and landed almost silently on the lump, (which turned out to be part of a sugar beet field). We stepped on to proper ground, at last, laughed, hugged and squinted at the sky when we heard a helicopter. Waving my arms and hockey stick above my head, I shouted, 'That helicopter's coming for us, Gran. Rescue at last!'

With the yellow bird approaching fast, we burst into silly-sounding laughter mixed with a dash of unsociable screaming. The chopper hovered right above, deafening us with its incredible mechanical roar. The force of the swirling blades, like a giant hairdryer, blew down, nearly pushing us over. It hovered, frozen in mid-air and a man in yellow dropped down to us on a strong wire.

'Another human being,' I cried. We were no longer the only people on earth.

Our hero introduced himself as Phil. He securely wrapped Gran in belts and straps which he clicked on to his own harness. 'I feel like a trussed-up piece of beef,' she shouted above the noise of the chopper.

'I'll come back for you, Miss, once I've settled your mum.'

'She's not my mum . . .' The rest of my sentence disappeared, gobbled up by the roar of the engine. I watched them rise up and up. Her dress flapped in the wind and water dripped from her one remaining slipper – a right one on a left foot.

As soon as I'd been raised into the chopper, I told Phil about the cow in the tree. He said, 'We don't do cows, but I'll put through a call to animal rescue.'

I took hold of my talisman and showed it to Phil. 'Are you my good luck hero who's come to save me?'

He smiled and said, 'I'm happy to have saved you, but I'm not your hero.'

I felt a bit disappointed and turned to glance at the drenched land below.

In minutes, we landed in a village hall car park on top of a giant H that someone had painted in white. Two old ladies shuffled over, wrapped us each in a massive towel and guided us into the hall. We scoffed delicious scones, jam and cream, chocolate Swiss roll, Madeira cake and ginger biscuits, washed down with mugs of steaming tea. Gran relaxed in happiness. And so did I (with a packet of jelly babies and an extra long sausage roll – don't tell Gran).

Later, dry and warm, while eating a fish and chips supper in the hall, I asked Gran what the "very important matter" was she wanted to tell me. She gave me one of her pitying looks with a tight-lipped, false smile – not like the Gran I knew. 'It's rather awkward, Deni. It's about leaving.'

'Do you mean leaving your home?'

‘No, Deni love, worse than that. I don’t know how to say it, even though I’ve been thinking about it for days.’ She waited a while and I too had to wait. I wished she’d hurry and say what she had to say. ‘The thing is Deni, while you were staying at my house, and I’m sorry to be the one that has to tell you, your lovely mum left your wonderful dad.’

Had the hall roof fallen down on my head? I couldn’t believe what Gran had just said. I stared through her, my mouth wide open and dried up like the Sahara desert. Words would not come out, even though I desperately wanted to speak. I grabbed my glass and swigged a large gulp of water, coughed and almost choked. ‘Mum left Dad and me? Do you mean for good?’

‘I think so, sweetheart.’

‘But why?’ I asked with a scowl. My fork slipped from my hand on to my plate splattering a blob of ketchup across the table.

‘She didn’t give a reason, pet. Sometimes unpleasantness happens in life and it’s often a mystery.’

Tears formed in my blurring eyes as Gran’s horrible words strangled my throat. I blinked rapidly. Gran leant across the table and put a hand on mine. ‘You’ll still live with your dad in the same house, and Chloe will be next door as always.’

I wanted her words to stop, but they kept coming. ‘You won’t need to move school.’

I banged the table with a fist. Cutlery jumped high and tingled as it crashed back down. Two or three people turned to glance at us. I peered up at Gran, feeling an increasing distance between us. ‘But you knew all along and you didn’t say anything.’

‘I couldn’t tell you earlier. Mum made me promise to keep quiet about it until she’d gone. If it were up to me I would have told you sooner, Deni, I promise I would.’

Aches in my chest and stomach seemed to arrive from nowhere adding to my increasing bad feeling. My heart boomed like a drummer thrashing. I felt weaker with every beat. ‘Why didn’t Mum tell me herself? ‘I suppose she couldn’t face up to your reaction . . . your disappointment.’

So, making me stay with Gran deliberately kept me out of the way while Mum packed and took off. After all, hadn’t she said there would be a big storm coming? Some storm *she* started. Maybe it should have been *our* house in the flood. Maybe the water might have surrounded us and we would’ve worked together to survive together and stay together.

‘You adults have a way of upsetting things.’

I didn’t want to eat or speak any more. I turned around and faced the wall, dragging my chair on the wooden floor with a screech loud enough to wake the buried dead in the cemetery next door. I placed my elbows on my knees and my upset, angry face in my hands. The world zoomed off behind me into the distance.

6 Ignored and Rejected

Once, at a Year 4 parent-evening interview, my class teacher spoke to my dad for five awful minutes before she realised her mistake. She told him, "Your daughter is no more than average at English." Then she noticed my frowning face, sat bolt upright and said, "What am I talking about? Deni is *brilliant* at English!" When my own teacher muddled me with someone else, that's being ignored. And I didn't like it.

Mum ignored me, big time. She sent me to Gran's with a purpose, while she slipped away, not to be seen since. Neither she nor Dad bothered to give me an explanation for her leaving. It remained a secret, a puzzle, a small mystery for me to solve. I didn't want to try and find her. I didn't imagine she wanted to be found. How much more could a mother ignore a daughter than by strolling off and not seeing her again? She never said goodbye. That hurt.

I'd been dishing out my own batch of ignoring – to my very good friend Chloe. And I've done it to her before. All I'd given her recently was an undeserved dose of rejection, sulkiness and moodiness. I neither asked her over nor sat with her on the school bus. Dad said, "You're showing upset at Mum leaving." But Mum or no Mum, I should never have treated Chloe so badly. I needed her and it couldn't have been any easier. She lived next door.

When one of us wanted the other's company, we'd use our secret method. We'd stick a large smiley face on our bedroom window and open it fully so that face could be seen by the other. That meant we were home and open for a visit. We created this system before we got our mobile phones and we kept it going, but it can be slow.

I hoped Chloe's window would be open, so I opened mine and leant out to check hers a few metres away to my left. It was wide open but confusing. There was no smiley face. Instead, staring back at me – a picture of a cow.

She'll be cross with me. She won't come over, ever. She hates me. I've lost my mum and I've lost my best friend.

Leaning out of the window, facing the cow, hope fading, I called, 'Chloe . . . can you . . . come over . . . please?'

Almost instantly, her window slammed shut with a huge bang. She had locked herself in and she had locked me out because I'd ignored her. It's what I should expect.I closed my window, sat at my desk, held my breath and listened. I heard Chloe through the wall, shuffling about inside her room. A drawer opening and closing, footsteps, a clinking sound, more footsteps, light switch, a door opened. She sprinted down her stairs two or three steps at a time and shouted, 'Bye Mum. Going to Deni's.' I felt the vibration of her front door as she pulled it shut behind her, leaving the letterbox flap rocking with a squeak.

Chloe's coming! Will she give me a hard time for rejecting her? Or will she forgive me?

Seconds later she crashed through our unlocked front door and called out, 'Hi, Mr T. It's me!' I sensed excitement in her few words.

Dad called back from the kitchen, 'Hi Chloe. Shoes off please.'

Leaving her shoes somewhere on the stairs, she bounded up two steps at a time and entered my room like a racing greyhound (permission given never to knock). At least she arrived with a gigantic smile but no eye contact. She had cake crumbs on her top and wore odd socks. Nothing unusual there. She plonked herself on my bed, faced the ceiling and stretched her legs up the wall. Her unbrushed, wavy brown hair spread over the side of the bed, reaching to the floor.

'Hiya, moody face,' she said.

I swivelled my chair round to face her. 'And what's with the cow picture?' I had to ask.

'That's you – for ignoring me all last week.'

'You're right. I have been an absolute cow, horns and all. I'm sorry . . .'

'I've been worried about you, you moo. And Mum's in a foul mood 'cause that greedy cat Drainpipe scoffed some sausages that were left out for supper.'

'That's weird you talking about *your* mum because I wanted to speak to you about *mine*. She's been gone two weeks and I'm nowhere near understanding why. After she left, I needed to be alone to sort out my head. I wanted to be invisible, but I also wanted attention. It's like opposites.'

Chloe gazed at the ceiling and drew circles in the air with her outstretched arms. 'Did anything unusual happen before your mum left?'

'I don't recall anything unusual. You know she sent me to Gran's deliberately to keep me out of the way while she made a quick exit. She'd planned her leaving in advance and didn't want me knowing anything about it.'

'Well, do you know what? I did hear something.'

I rolled my chair nearer to Chloe. 'What do you mean?'

'I think it could've been the week before your mum left. I was downstairs reading on my own, when I heard a door slam in your front room, then voices. You know how nosey I am. I stuck my ear to the wall and listened to your parents arguing. She said he'd "wasted it all."'

'Really? Wasted what all?'

'Your mum said that your dad is always collecting rubbishy things that cost a lot.' She giggled. 'He's like a schoolboy – he'll be doing Bring and Tell next!'

Chloe's legs waved about above the bed. She kicked my Star Wars poster off its Blu-tak. It slid downwards and she pinned it against the wall with a foot.

'Dad does collect stuff,' I said. 'Dinosaur bones! He spends loads of cash at car boots and on eBay buying fossilised mammoth ribs, T-rex thighs and brontosaurus teeth. He told me he'd make pots of money selling them in the future. I think you're right. Mum could have been angry and upset with Dad wasting money in that way.'

'But do you think that's a reason to walk out on you?' she asked while Blu-tacking my poster back up, slightly skew-whiff.

'Money is important and Dad's obsessed with collecting stuff – he can't help himself. He spends ages on the internet hoping to add expensive items to his collections.'

'I'd leave my husband if ever he wasted our money like that,' Chloe said.

'What husband? No one's going to marry you, Chloe.' We giggled and I said, 'Did you know, my dad has a collection of over fifty "nearly round" stones? The biggest one cost him thirty pounds!'

'Stones? You're joking!'

'I hardly ever see him. He ignores me. He spends all his time on those lousy collections. I'm not going to feel guilty about Mum leaving because *he* drove her away. I didn't.'

I started to sweat a bit. 'Dad's to blame for all this mess, I'm certain.' Blaming him made me feel better straight away. 'I'm planning to put him in a care home.'

Chloe rolled on to her stomach and stretched her neck in order to see me. 'Don't be upset, Deni. She'll come back, maybe when your dad sorts himself out.'

'She won't. She's taken all her clothes, CDs and cooking stuff. She's moved out all right. I bet her stuff is more valuable to her than I am right now. Ignored and rejected, that's me.'

'You're not loved, dearie, that's your trouble. But I love you!' And she made a goofy teeth face. 'We're still best mates, ain't we, Deni?'

'Course we are. I'm sorry.'

I leant over to Chloe, we clasped hands and she twisted mine until I fell off my chair.

The bully in our class, Dirk Watchett, at the age of six, put a worm up his nose. It wriggled deep into his head and he was operated on at the hospital. I think it must have eaten half of his brain because he does the craziest things.

At the age of nine, he was sent home for pulling down the TV room curtains and cutting them up to make a Batman cloak. And he ruined our Year 6 trip to Banham Zoo.

We were on the coach returning to school from the zoo when Mr Slugge (nickname ‘Slimy’) came up to the back of the coach to investigate a funny smell. Someone said Danny Mulhouse had been eating pomegranate seeds again. Slimy ignored that and inspected all our shoes. He toppled from seat to seat and sniffed the soles of every shoe and trainer. He didn’t find the source of the pong.

“Open your bags,” he insisted. Watchett unzipped his school bag and out flapped a duck. It quacked and flew madly up and down the coach, and must have been very frightened. Most of us screamed as the panic-stricken mallard swooped over our heads. Loose feathers scattered about the coach, got sucked into the air conditioning system, chewed up and blown out on to our heads. Feathers drifted everywhere – a scene from one of those glitter-filled, shake-it-and-see globes. ‘It’s snowing,’ cried Danny Mulhouse.

The poor duck flew up and down, up and down the coach, not knowing what it should do or how to escape. It arrived at the front of the coach and flapped around the driver’s face. The driver shouted, ‘Someone grab that blinkin’ bird.’

Slimy dived at the creature as it passed overhead but failed to catch it. The duck pooed on Slimy’s bald head then landed exhausted on the driver's shoulder, where it slept for the rest of the journey.

Watchett was nearly expelled for; (a) kidnapping a wild animal, (b) imprisoning it in a bag without sufficient air supply, and (c) causing it to poo on a teacher's head. Since that incident, I think Watchett has been very frightened of birds of any kind.

There's a rumour still going around the school that Slimy roasted the duck for his supper and ate it with some orange sauce.

At break the following day, Chloe and I cornered Watchett in the playground. For once he was without his gang. 'We don't want you hanging around us, making false comments about Deni's trips and stuff,' Chloe told him. 'We're getting bored of you.'

Watchett faced me. He chewed the side of his thumb and looked around for any members of his gang. 'I'll say what I want,' said Watchett. 'I bet your dad wouldn't talk like that to his *new girlfriend.*'

I grabbed Watchett by his sweatshirt, knowing it was not the right thing to do, but he was asking for it. He knew how to wind me up. 'What are you saying, bulldog lips?'

'I saw him in a café in the city, having coffee with this strange woman. They chatted for ages – and your dad paid the bill.'

It was his smiling I detested. It showed he enjoyed his attacks. 'Clear off, Watchett. I don't need your silly lies.'

He dipped into his pocket and took out a small, crinkled envelope. 'Look in here.'

I took the envelope. 'It's April – a bit late for a Christmas card.'

'Just open it,' he insisted.

I let go of his sweatshirt with a slight push. Watchett trotted off, straightening his crumpled clothes. He shouted to us, 'Ask your dad if you don't believe me. Perhaps that's why your mum ran off!'

I opened the envelope and took out a poor quality, fuzzy photo of a café, taken from the street. Dad sat at the café window talking to a woman but her face remained hidden behind a poster stuck on the window. COFFEE AND CAKE OFFER – TWO FOR ONE.

Chloe put an arm around my shoulders. 'Do as Watchett suggests – ask your dad. Otherwise, we'll never know.'

'Dad doesn't like to talk about Mum and her leaving and all that stuff, but if he is seeing someone new, we'll need to keep a close eye on him.'

7 Wedding Ring Fling

Dad and I were out in the back garden. In an effort to be friendly and fatherly he said, 'Let's play a game of short tennis.'

'I *hate* stupid short tennis,' I responded sharply, snapping at him with the *hate*. I didn't want to show any form of weakness by doing him any favours. But, seeing he'd got all the equipment out and had set the net up, I eventually agreed to a knock-around.

After playing for a while, I began to enjoy the exercise. I whacked the sponge ball and made it difficult for Dad to hit, but he played well until he suddenly stopped and froze as if he'd been turned into a stone statue.

'My gold ring! My wedding ring! Where is it?' he cried, looking intensely at his bare finger, then frantically at the ground. 'It must have dropped off during our game.'

I forced myself to show some interest. 'Are you sure you had it on?'

'I'm never without it, am I?'

'How should I know?' I grumped.

'Help me find it, Deni.' And he knelt down.

With serious concentration on his face and misery on mine, we searched and searched, faster and faster, flicking through the grass, flowers and shrubs with our tennis rackets. Dad chopped wildly, hacking the pink tulips with his racket, not caring if he swiped off their flowers. All that destruction left a herby fragrance floating in the air. Had he forgotten that Mum planted those tulips a few years ago?

Minutes later, as I pretended to search, I spotted the ring glistening in the long grass at the edge of the lawn. Rather than tell Dad I'd found it, I grabbed it and when he had his back to me I buried it in the soil and stamped a heap of dirt down hard over it.

'Found it, Deni?' he asked, watching over his shoulder.

'No – false alarm! I'm killing a wasp!'

I thought, he doesn't need a wedding ring if he has no wife to love. ("With this ring, I thee wed.")

He carried on searching for his precious ring until it got dark and I'd gone to bed without saying goodnight,

(which didn't feel as bad as leaving home without saying goodbye.)

Lying in bed, I thought about his collecting habit, money and Mum leaving and wondered if they were linked. What reward did he get from hoarding all that junk? Did he really waste our money on his collecting hobby? Could money have been important enough to have made Mum leave? Is he really seeing someone else? That *would* have given Mum reason for running off.

At bedtime, he came to tuck me in and I went straight to the point. 'Your collecting hobby – how did it all start?'

'I must admit,' he said, as he sat down on my bed, 'our family has always collected and I get it from them. My granddad collected helmets during the war. He had helmets from every country except one – Japan. On the boat back to England, he met this bloke who said he had a Japanese helmet for sale that once belonged to a general. Granddad paid a whole week's wages for it.'

I yawned and Dad pulled my quilt up and tucked it under my chin. He could be quite caring sometimes. 'Did that complete his helmet collection?'

'No. It turned out not to be a Japanese helmet at all but a common motorcyclist's helmet. You could pick them up for a few pence. Granddad got a serious telling-off from his wife when she found out he'd wasted a whole week's wages in one go.'

'I bet she went mad at him – as Mum did with you.' I cuddled Garlic Breath tightly.

'Don't go there, Deni.'

'I don't want to collect stuff as you do, Dad. But I'm going to have a souvenirs box.'

'Forget collecting. Stick to doing your silly pranks.'

It was late and my tired eyes would not easily stay open. 'What silly pranks?'

'You're always playing jokes. Remember when I went away on business and you put fine plaster paste into the open end of my toothpaste tube and let it dry rock hard? I never realised why my toothpaste couldn't be squeezed!'

I laughed.

'You're a bit of a joker, you are, Deni. But some of your so-called jokes go a bit too far.'

'Tell me, tell me,' I said, beginning to feel more awake.

'That April Fool when you put an old bird's nest in the collar of my shirt which had been hanging overnight on the clothesline. You remember. You called out, "A bird's built a nest in your shirt!" I dashed outside to see the nest, shocked that such a fine thing could be made by a bird. I phoned the local newspaper and they ran a story on it for days, with photos.'

'I remember that.' I smiled, enjoying our conversation.

He stood up to go, leant over and kissed my forehead and Garlic Breath, as he always did. 'There's a sad side to you Deni, and I think you blame me for Mum leaving. These past months have been a struggle, haven't they? But I'm determined to involve you more in my life.'

My eyes closed again. 'Involve me more in what?'

'My new job finding film sites, because it involves going around the world, I want you to come along too. You enjoyed Brazil. It'll be an adventure and an education, and maybe a good way of us getting closer and understanding each other better. You're growing up so fast – soon you'll be thirteen.'

‘Sounds good,’ I muttered, too tired to understand fully what he had said.

That night I dreamed of stretching my arms out and flying high around the world, like Superwoman. I didn’t recognise myself up in the swirling clouds, diving and twisting, overtaking planes and dodging space stations. Instead, I saw Mum as Superwoman. I became panicky and short of breath and I shouted and shouted, ‘Come down, Mum. You can’t fly.’

She either didn’t hear me or she refused to listen.

8 My Souvenir Box

Chloe relaxed cross-legged on my bedroom floor, arms folded, hair in bunches, feet in pale blue flip-flops. She had burst into my room a minute ago smiling and headed directly to my private sweet cupboard. She dropped the smile on seeing it empty but for half a stale Hobnob, which she ate.

With a mouth full of dry biscuit, she spluttered, 'I've noticed something strange.' She swallowed the food. 'You have a painting of a mountain scene in your hallway, right?'

'Right. It's a view in the Lake District.'

'Well, "detective Tutting," go downstairs and take a look at it, would you?'

I did as she asked and returned with a question. 'Did you knock it off the wall when you rushed in? There's just the nail and dust marks where the frame used to hang.'

'I didn't knock it. Guess where it is?'

'In a charity shop.'

'No. It's in my house!'

I moved closer to her. 'Are you for real? The very same one?'

'It's on my mum's bedroom wall. I saw it this morning when I took her a cup of tea.'

'Do you think my Dad gave it to her?'

'He must have – unless she stole it.'

'Maybe it's a birthday gift.'

'Her birthday's in January.'

'Could this mean your mum is the mystery woman in the café, and they're having secret meetings?' I asked.

'It's called a *rendezvous*. I read about it in Mum's Cosmopolitan.'

'We'll have to ask Watchett and show him a photo of your mum to see if he recognises her.'

'I'll trawl through my photos – I've loads on my mobile. Did you get a chance to ask your Dad about the woman in the café?'

'No. Let's try your idea first and show Watchett a picky of your mum.'

Chloe leant forward and turned her attention to something under my bed. Hitting the object with a fist, she asked, 'What's with the pet coffin?'

'That's my souvenir box. Got the idea from Gran. She stores all her treasures in an old hat box.'

I joined her on the floor, hair in ponytail, feet in squirrel slippers. From under the bed, I hauled out a heavy wooden chest and brushed off a small cobweb on one of the sides. 'It's Dad's old toolbox. I took it.'

It had an old-fashioned appearance – a well-used box, solidly made, that had lived a useful life before I got hold of it. On the lid faint letters could be seen – *BILL TURNER'S FRESH BUTTER* – over-painted many times. Its coating of varnish had started to peel off in places, like sunburned skin, revealing paint layers showing it had once been red and then green.

'Padlocked I see. And what's that label taped to the side?' Chloe moved in for a closer view. 'KEEP OUT, PRIVATE.' Then she covered one eye with a hand and, in a poor imitation of a pirate added, 'Ah-har, matey. Be it full-o-treasure? King's gold.'

I had to laugh. 'You're crazy.'

'Maybe crazy but I'm happy.'

I undid the padlock and lifted the lid, which let out a slight squeak from a rusty hinge. Inside, not much to show but a rotten smell of drains made a nasty first impression. 'Just a few things – the start of a special collection. Some people collect glass animals or wargame figures. Well, I don't.' I said, a bit embarrassed at the lack of items.

'It's not blinking treasure, is it?' Chloe asked, screwing her face up at the emptiness. She liked surprises and must have felt disappointed.

'Souvenirs, that's all.'

'Souvenirs of what?' she asked.

'Souvenirs of my trips and stuff.'

'Well, you haven't been on many trips, have you? So you wouldn't expect to have collected many souvenirs, would you?' And she dived in and pulled out Joey the donkey. 'I remember this. We used to play "stables" at playschool.'

'Yeah, that's Joey,' I said, thrilled that Chloe recognised him. 'Thought it would be a reminder of us as buddies.'

I pulled out the smelly object. 'Gran's mud-covered slipper from the big flood.?

'What? Do you still have that mouldy old thing? No wonder your box stinks of drains.'

'It reminds me of what happened and how I saved her from the flood. It's evidence. I couldn't keep the bathtub as a souvenir, could I?'

From the bottom of the box, I picked up a circus entrance ticket. 'And this is from a memorable trip to the circus, aged five . . .'

'That doesn't look anything special,' she interrupted.

'. . . with my mum.'

She paused for a few seconds and frowned. 'Sorry, Deni. I didn't mean to make fun or anything.' She touched me on the shoulder. 'Keepsakes should be personal and respected. I know that.'

She explored deeper inside the box and took out another item which had been hiding in a corner. 'Your Brazilian drinking straw. Get lost killer bee.' She blew down it, making rude noises by squeezing the end.'

We fell on to our backs, laughed and thumped the bedroom floor until Dad shouted up the stairs. 'You two OK?'

'Fine, Mr Tutting,' Chloe shouted back, elbowing me in the arm. She threw the drinking straw back into the box.

'As a souvenir box, it's a start I suppose. As you go on more trips you'll be able to collect all sorts of things like painted shells, baseball caps, toilet roll covers . . .'

'Thanks for those suggestions . . . not. Each item has its story, and you know how much I love telling stories.'

'Why don't you keep your lucky half medal in there too?'

'I'm supposed to wear it always for when my secret rescuer turns up.'

‘Well, they didn’t turn up in Brazil. Are you sure you’re not copying your dad and starting to collect stuff as the rest of the Tuttings have done since time began?’

‘It’s not the same – I don’t spend any money!’

‘Mmm, just checking.’

Chloe made a banana-shaped smile, took hold of Joey the donkey and galloped him around the floor, as though we were back in playschool.

After she left, I plodded downstairs like a zombie to see what Dad had tried to burn for tea. I smelled disaster. With my arms stretched out before me, I entered the kitchen. ‘I come for your blood,’ I said in my best vampire voice. But instead of biting Dad on the neck I was forced to cough. A smoky pong of scorched crumpets hit my nose like a door smashing into my face.

He stood over the sink, knife in hand, scraping the burnt bits off a slab of blackened crumpet. I asked, ‘How many minutes did you toast those crumpets for? They normally take two.’

‘Sixteen,’ he replied.

‘Sixteen minutes? That’s mad.’ (The most amazing fact about crumpets is – no matter how much you burn them the little holes in the crumpet will always be there.)

‘For your cooking skills, I give you zero out of ten this week. Animals get tastier meals than I do. I’d eat pigswill. It’s a million times tastier than rock hard crumpets.’

Dad and I met at the kitchen table surrounded by crumpet fog. He threw down a plate of black rocky chunks. ‘There’s your supper – it’s the best I can do.’

I grabbed a hammer and chisel and trimmed off the blackened sides, tops and bases of my crumpets, only to be left staring at a few minuscule pieces of squidgy dough, like chewing gum. I couldn’t eat any of it. A warm bowl of fish blood would have satisfied me more.

I'd even drink pigeon milk rather than eat his food. 'You'll have to admit it Dad, you are a failed cook.'

'Yeh, cooking just doesn't like me.' He fanned the fog with his apron and it began to clear. I found a few microwaveable mini-pizzas in the freezer so we had those instead.

Watchett's words in the playground suddenly came back into my head . . . "Ask him if you don't believe me. Perhaps that's why your mum ran off!"

The moment felt right to ask, though I couldn't be one hundred per cent sure about Dad. His reactions were not always that easy to predict.

'Dad, with Mum gone and all that, do you think you'll start going out with a new woman?'

'Oh, not that business again, crikey.' He slapped a tea towel across the table, making me shudder. 'Deni, I do *not* want to discuss my private married life with my own daughter, thank you!'

I had better change the subject of our conversation yet again. However, as I went to speak . . . 'Have you thought any more about what you'd like for your thirteenth birthday?' He sat at the table with a pencil and paper.

'I'd like a puppy.'

'We're not having a dog. I'll be the mug who'll end up walking it, feeding it and bagging up its poos.'

He's being mean now. 'I'd do my share, cut his nails and brush him.'

'How do you know it'll be a he?'

'Because I'm gonna call him Benedict.'

'No dog's gonna come to a call of "Benedict." And don't you need to see the dog before you name it, see its character?'

'I suppose so.' I wasn't making any progress with the puppy thing. 'What about a hamster?'

'They only come out at night.'

'They're nocturnal.'

'Which means I'll be up all hours and have to feed and clean it while you're snoring away in bed.'

'A snake then.' He squirmed a bit.

'They're always escaping.'

'A week-old crocodile.'

'It'll grow to six metres.'

'Oh, forget about pets, Dad. My birthday's months away anyhow. Why don't we go on another trip soon?' I added a few supporting claps.

'You sound keen. I happen to be arranging one at the moment, to a tropical island.'

'That'll be great. I could bring back a palm tree but I won't fit it into my souvenir box.'

'There'll be fabulous seashells. You could collect them.'

'Can Chloe come?'

'Afraid not – insurance nightmare.'

Of course he wouldn't take her. I firmly pushed aside my plate of volcanic bits and stood up to go.

'Oh, I almost forgot – Gran's got something for you. I'll drop you off there if you like.'

Our car pulled up and Gran appeared at the back door, drying her hands on her apron. Since the flood, we'd not seen each other. (She stayed at her sister's while the house had its make-over.)

She hobbled over to the car and spoke through the window. 'Hi you two,' she said with a giggle. 'Will you stay for cake, Tony? It's jam sponge, your favourite.'

'No thanks, Mum. Going to the supermarket. Be back in an hour to pick Deni up, if that's all right.'

I jumped out of the car and waved Dad goodbye. He tooted the horn as he disappeared through the open gate.

Gran and I squeezed each other tightly in an eye-popping embrace. 'Come see my new furniture and floors, and the bath – it's white!'

She showed me her replacement flood-proof doors, explaining how they worked. All the holes that had let the flood water in had been closed up. The washed-off plaster had been replaced and painted. It all appeared tidy and fresh. Her new furniture fitted in perfectly and looked modern compared with her old worn out brown stuff. The smell of paint and new wood in the air had kicked out the stench of rotten water.

'I'm prepared for the next river explosion,' she said.

'Well, keep that hockey stick handy.' We laughed.

The jam sponge tickled my taste buds. I ate two pieces and Dad's slice as well.

'I've got a little something for you, Deni. Just a small gift for all your help during the flood.' She toddled over to the new oak kitchen dresser and fetched a book-sized object wrapped in brown paper.

'What's this, Gran?'

'Open it and see, lovey.'

I winced when she handed it to me – another surprise. It didn't feel like a book. I opened the package quickly and took out a framed photograph of Dad, Mum and me taken when I was about five.

I smiled and gave Gran a tight squeeze. 'Thanks, Gran.' But it made me think about secrets and Mum leaving and flooded rooms and fields and drowned animals – scenes I would rather forget.

On our return journey, I pretended to sleep so I wouldn't have to speak to Dad and get shouted at for mentioning Mum.

Arriving home, I dashed from the car before the engine had been switched off, and sprinted up the stairs three steps at a time. Dad shouted after me, ‘What did Gran give you?’

‘A photograph,’ I shouted back, not wanting him to see it.

I dumped the framed photo in my souvenir box, slammed down the lid and padlocked it.

Tight.

9 A Fishy Tale

On the morning of our school story-telling event, Chloe came around to collect me for the bus as usual. Dad would not come to hear me speak, so he didn't get his goodbye kiss. "Important work up north," he'd said. What an excuse. He should have been there with me, for me. I wanted his support. I wanted him to see me on stage. I didn't want any more rejection and I didn't want to be ignored.

I slammed the front door behind me. Was that a shout of "good luck" coming from the kitchen? I couldn't be sure.

A low fog was just clearing from the Village Green leaving behind a sharp autumn chill in the air. We pulled our coats on as we neared the bus stop. 'Is your mum coming?' I asked Chloe.

'She can't make it, but I'm not bothered.'

'I'm not the only one who gets ignored then. Dad's not coming. I hope Dad and your mum are not staying in for some "going out. We hardly spoke during the twenty-minute bus ride to school. Instead, we read over our notes and made corrections. I imagined myself standing on that broad stage with its massive red velvet curtains. Spotlights, the size of dustbins, will shine down on me. I'll be a star for a day.

Mr Woodlouse, the 'new' Head of English ('new'– even though he'd been at the school for eight years), had created the story-telling event. "Miss Tutting," he told me a few weeks ago, "It's a chance for pupils such as yourself, who enjoy speaking in public, to have a go in front of a real audience – the whole school."

Posters about the event appeared on walls all over the school. No pupil could miss seeing at least one on the way to class.

CREATIVE STORY-TELLING EXTRAVAGANZA!

DO YOU HAVE AN AMAZING STORY TO TELL?

THEN TAKE A FART IN FRONT OF THE WHOLE SCHOOL

Yes, it had a spelling mistake, but that wasn't the reason why I pulled down every poster I came across. Ripped them right off the walls and tore them to shreds. On *every one* of them, in thick black marker pen, someone had scrawled, *"Deni Tutting loves telling lies."*

Chloe picked up a poster. 'I can tell his scribble anywhere. See the "o" in "loves?" Watchett writes his o like a six.'

'They do look like sixes, but why is Watchett so annoying, calling me a liar? I should report him.'

‘That turnip deserves a clout if he trashes your story.’

‘Or yours. You’re very brave telling your *Vampire Millionaire story*. I’m proud of you.’

(Her story centred around a millionaire who pays to get bitten by a vampire, turns into one and then opens a private school so that she can infect unfortunate children and change them into vampires. I was quite surprised and pleased with Chloe’s effort. She’d always found creative writing a bit of a struggle. However, she read it to me, and after a few changes, it was ready for the world to hear.)

‘I’m dead scared,’ I admitted to Chloe as we hovered at the side of the stage like two flapping butterflies. ‘I know my jitters will disappear once I start speaking. I learned that much from my last effort in front of the class.’

‘You’ll be okay, you will. You’ve given talks before and you’ve got lots of natural confidence when you speak in public. It’s one of your talents – along with choosing me as a best friend.’ She slapped me on the back of my head. ‘You love all that attention.’

‘Will *they* like it though – those pupils, teachers and parents?’

‘Just pretend you’re in your own bedroom talking to me. Your nerves will soon vanish,’ she said. ‘If I can force a giggle or two out of that lot out there, I’d be happy!’

‘Yours might be a laugh ‘cause you’re a funny stand-up comedian, but mine’s a near tragedy.’

‘Speaking of tragedies, here comes our poster scribbler,’ Chloe said and nodded in the direction of the gang of four creeping up behind me. A smell of mouldy socks gave a clue and I turned to face Dirk Watchett and three of his apes.

'Got another pack of lies for us, Tutting?' he asked, smirking to his unwashed gang of losers. 'Can't wait to hear how you escaped from the two-inch blood-sucking worm. It must have been *so* frightening for you.' He danced like a wriggling maggot and his trio giggled and high-fived. Watchett flashed his ultra-white teeth, which I know he cleans with Toilet Duck.

Chloe switched to bulldozer mode. Keeping her voice soft so she wouldn't be heard by the audience, she told him, 'We'd rather escape *from* a worm than to actually *be* one. You just watch it, Watchett, in case I tread on you or a little bird gobbles you up.' And with the *you* she pointed at his face. He squirmed and quietly backed off because he feared Chloe. She could act tough when required and once she pinched him.

'And thanks for your comments on the posters – all publicity is useful,' I said. He grinned and opened out his hands as if to say, "How else can I help?"

The headteacher passed in a hurry, dragging by her wrist a Year 4 girl with a nosebleed. Without stopping, the head asked Watchett, 'Shouldn't you be in the audience?' So, Watchett and his crew wandered off without further pestering to grab seats somewhere near the exit at the back of the hall, ready for a quick getaway. Maybe they'll boo me or shout nasty comments.

We seemed to be hanging about for ages waiting to get on stage. Every glance I took at the big round clock told the same time! Chloe had even longer to wait – she was on after me.

On the stage, Timothy Fuller-Tatt began to stammer and lose his way. While in the audience, two parent-governors and head of geography, Mrs Sandy, got up and stormed out of the hall, blowing out their cheeks.

Seeing them leave made me jittery. I couldn't imagine how Fuller-Tatt was feeling.

'Look, Chloe. Fuller-Tatt has finally run out of words. He's giving up.'

Showing a face like a hissing cat, he almost sprinted off stage to a dozen or so claps. His presentation, *Tin Mining – A Cornwall Story of Toil,* may have been a bit too technical for most of the pupils in the audience.

Replacing Fuller-Tatt at the microphone, an agitated Mr Woodlouse squinted in my direction and beckoned. 'Hurry up, girl,' he hissed. 'We're running late.' That caused me to fumble a bit and I almost dropped my notes.

'Good luck,' Chloe said, pushing me up the creaking steps to the stage. 'Sock it to 'em.'

I plodded towards the microphone, like a donkey on Scarborough beach, hardly paying any attention to Mr Woodlouse's introduction. 'Ladies and gentlemen, boys and girls, here to report on her latest holiday mishap – give it up for Deni Tutting, Year 8.'

A half-hearted round of applause followed and someone shouted, 'It's all made up!' I pretended to know who had called out and I smiled and waved in their direction. Mr Woodlouse waddled off stage still clapping after everyone else had stopped.

I scanned the hall, not looking anyone directly in the eye. But very little could be seen because the stage lights, set very low down, shone right into my face. I shuffled forwards and backwards a few times before I found a suitable spot clear of the bright light.

Someone shouted, 'Get on with it.' I tried to smile but failed. Can't people wait quietly?

'Go on, Deni,' Danny Mulhouse called out from the front row.

'Don't encourage her!' someone else blurted.

Then a strict 'Shhh!' finally produced silence.

Little me, on such an enormous stage – no longer Deni Tutting – but a performer ready to entertain. I faced the crowd, focused on a distant spot and tried to ignore all the eyes – staring, questioning, expecting.

In my sweaty left hand, the elastic waistband did not make much of an impression. It was a twisted, knotted and shrivelled loop of material; not much to look at. I raised it up over my head and shouted as loud as I dared, 'This piece of elastic . . . saved my life!'

I began my story.

Dad and I held tightly on the railings at the front of a massive yacht called Sea-Ya. The water sprayed our faces with a cooling mist as the boat rocked up and down. We sailed towards an uninhabited island to do some filmmaking. 'Are there any sharks in the Australian sea, Dad?'

'Loads. That's why the captain said we can't swim or go fishing. Sharks on a hook can flip up out of the water and bite off a fisherman's head!'

'This'll be a great trip then if we have to keep watching out for hungry sharks!'

'Well, you did ask.'

'How long are we on the boat?'

'One night going, one night back.'

'Anyone famous?'

'There are five actors, a film crew and the guys running the ship. I don't think you'd know them, but it's a big movie. *Alien Pirates Search for a Lost Treasure Temple but Stumble Across Giant Mutant Ants!*'

'That's definitely the worst and longest film title ever in the history of ridiculous film titles.'

'Big movie – big title!'

I had my own tiny room, with a porthole, a diddy sink, mini-fridge and mouse-size cupboards. I also had the luxury of a rocking hammock that stretched across the cabin. The first time I attempted to lie in it, it tipped me over and out on to the floor. Seven goes it took before I was able to lie steady.

Permission was given by Captain Blademan to roam freely around the boat. I enjoyed being on deck most of all. Miles of rope, long wooden poles, wheels, brass pulleys and tall sails rattled and clattered in the wind. I even steered the boat once we'd reached the open sea. Laughing dolphins followed alongside.

During supper, I asked Dad, 'What'll we do all evening? There's no TV.'

'We're all meeting on deck for snacks, drinks and story-telling. Should be enjoyable. They say Captain Blademan tells a good tale.'

'Your tales are enjoyable, Dad. Will you be telling a story?'

'I think I might have one to entertain everybody tonight. I met a queen some years ago . . .'

' . . . A real queen?'

'A *real* queen.'

We were interrupted by the arrival of my third dessert and, as food comes first, I stopped talking. A quick check to make sure it's what I ordered; a double chocolate sponge with warmed white chocolate sauce and dark chocolate fish-shaped sprinkles. (No cream in case I put on weight!)

Later, in a sleepy and relaxed mood on deck, Dad told his story about saving the queen. The listeners sat around, legs covered by blankets, sipping "Ozzy beer." I drank lemonade. 'I liked that story a lot, Dad, especially when you found the queen.' Again, I had to ask, 'Are you sure she's real?'

‘Oh, she’s a genuine, real living queen. I’d say she’s a living legend and I should get in touch with her, but that’s difficult in her country. They don’t have internet over there.’

Dad’s story engaged me so much that I hadn’t noticed yellow and red Chinese lanterns had been lit and placed all over the deck. They gave a warming glow and a delicate perfume. While Dad spoke, day turned gently into night.

Feeling tired, I let out a foghorn yawn, quickly followed by a *good night* to all on deck. The last thing I wanted was to watch grown-ups (or *groan* ups) moaning about adult stuff like politics, pensions and parenting.

Somehow I reached my cabin, climbed into my hammock without brushing my teeth, and fell asleep.

The following morning I woke early. I couldn’t sleep any longer because of Dad snoring like a hippo next door. His bedroom door rattled. I quietly put on a clean white T-shirt, yellow and blue shorts and a pair of flip-flops and went up on deck for a refreshing gulp of salty air. A warm breeze ruffled my hair and I felt the early rising sun on my skin. A lone seagull, perched on the railing at the front of the boat, flew off when it saw me. It shrieked like a child’s guitar out of tune, turned in the air and dived at my head, shrieking again. I ducked to avoid being hit. As the loony bird whizzed past, its black, piercing eyes almost hypnotised me. You don’t realise how enormous seagulls are until you’re right next to one.

The night watchman didn’t appear to be on duty when I glanced in his direction. He must have gone to bed early. I guessed Sea-Ya could drive itself if it had been set to automatic.

I heard a loud splash on the right side, the starboard, and suspected dolphins or sharks. I flip-flopped to the railings and squinted at the low, rising sun that shone directly into my face. As I looked out for signs of wildlife a sudden boat wobble caused a low pole to swing around and thump me forcefully on the back. I was knocked off my feet and flipped right over the top of the starboard guard railing. My whole back slammed against the side of the boat. I still had a firm grip on the railing, but I dangled on the outside of the boat like a decoration on a Christmas tree. One flip-flop remained on my right foot. The other must have been dropped on deck.

What if I let go? (You'd fall into the sea.) Were there any sharks, whales or giant squid waiting to gobble me up? (Yes, loads.) Will my hero save me? (Unlikely. You left your lucky half medal in your cabin.)

I screamed and banged my heels on the side of the boat, hoping someone would hear.

I hung on firmly but my grip had started to weaken already. 'Dad! Dad!'

I felt my grasp on the bar slip even further. I kicked and skidded against the slippery side of the boat but couldn't push my body upwards. It seemed a long way down to the water. 'Girl overboard!' I yelled.

The out of tune squawking returned. That crazy gull swooped and pecked at my fingers. I was forced to let go of the railing with my right hand leaving me holding on with only the left. The bird swooped again, this time pecking at my hair. I tried to head-butt it and failed. 'Get lost pigeon-face,' didn't do much to scare it either.

I couldn't believe what happened next. Pigeon-face pecked the flip-flop from my foot and flew off with it! I even imagined Dirk Watchett owned the seagull and had trained it to steal flip-flops.

I glanced at the deck, willing Dad to appear, but there was no sign of life. My right hand felt sore and was bleeding from the pecking. Drops of blood fell into the sea. (I read somewhere that sharks can detect blood in water miles away?)

I think I screamed when I let go of the railing and plunged into the grey morning sea, as cool as a fizzy drink. Screaming underwater was just a waste of time. The boat's twirling propeller hummed as it passed by, almost swallowing up my spreading hair.

My arms slashed the water as I dragged myself to the surface, spat out some poisonous salty water tasting of crabsticks and vinegar.

I gulped air. My lungs felt as though a wardrobe had fallen on them.

Sea-Ya lived up to its name and had already travelled too far to swim after, moving further away every second, leaving me flapping and thrashing about, desperate and helpless. I called, 'Help! It's Deni. I'm overboard.' But that was a waste of breath. Why hadn't that night watchman been on duty? He'd have spotted me straight away.

How long could I stay afloat without a lifejacket? Dad'll kill me for not wearing one. They have whistles. I might have been able to attract attention with a whistle. That could have saved me. And wasn't I always being told? "Wear your lifejacket on deck."

Keeping my head above the water and not getting cold became my top two aims. Treading water kept me on the surface, but I couldn't do it forever – till I was thirteen, twenty or fifty! I spun around searching for any floating object I could hold on to but found nothing.

There was a splash and I turned to see a dark, pointed dorsal fin cutting through the surface. A shark. I shivered at the thought and struggled to catch my breath. I heard my own heart beating faster and faster.

That monster fish circled around me – a dark, threatening shadow from the deep. At one point its tail brushed my shoulder as it whizzed past. I felt it was staring at me, and with its growing hunger and gnashing teeth I could be its next breakfast, lunch and supper all dished up on one plate. I was becoming one of a shark's *five a day*.

I continued treading water. When the shark dived I'd kick out violently. But aren't sharks attracted to movement? Perhaps I should stay still.

Then the creature passed without even a ripple, checking me out again, I noticed it had a long saw for a nose – like a chainsaw. It's a sawfish, not a shark! Was that good? The word *unfriendly* came to mind. I knew sawfish could detect food through sensors in the saw – in hundreds of tiny sharp teeth that edged its rim. I knew I'd rather tango with the Loch Ness Monster than waltz with this cross-eyed torpedo.

Staying afloat used up most of my energy. I had to stay alert too. I twisted my neck this way and that, spun around and dived, trying to see from where the scaly man-eater might attack. Then there would be moments of no movement, no sign of life, nothing except the vast, never-ending sea. Only the sound of my panic breathing and frantic splashing disturbed the silence. That thing lurking in the deep sea focused its killing skills firmly on me and it took all the time it needed.

I waved to the distant boat, dreadfully fearing I wouldn't ever be on board it again. No one waved back at me. I remained alone.

Twirling around, I spotted the crafty creature coming at me again at great speed, this time slashing and cutting the water with its deadly weapon, ready to chop me into bite-sized pieces; not fish fingers but *human* fingers! It was just showing off its weaponry. So I showed him mine – I waggled my fist. 'And I've got teeth!'

Quiet and stillness returned. I didn't like the quiet. This fish knew how to wait for its dinner. I hoped the killer had gone to pester some mackerel or a sardine. But, some way off, in a flash of silver and grey, it began to charge straight at me, doing its slashing and cutting thing. I had about a dozen seconds to prepare for impact.

One single idea came to mind. From my shorts I pulled out the elastic waistband and quickly tied the ends together to form a loop. I placed the loop around my ankles to make a catapult. Just as the fish charged at full speed, I lifted my feet out of the water and caught the tip of its saw in my catapult. The force of the attack stretched the elastic and launched the slimy fish backwards and upwards into space (more accurately, about five metres!)

I guess it did not like being out of the water, but do fish scream? I'm sure I heard the sawfish version of "Aaarrrggg!" He clearly had a sad expression. I've seen sad fish faces in trays at Tesco, surrounded by ice.

As I prepared my catapult for a possible second attack, Sea-Ya had managed to creep up behind me and a blast of its hooter nearly made me jump out of the water. I waved. The joy at seeing my boat was overwhelming. I think I cried. Through a loud hailer, Dad shouted, 'I'll chuck in a lifebuoy. Don't go anywhere.' Was he serious?

'Hurry Dad. I think it's circling for a second attack.'

Dad appeared above me and lowered a large rubber ring on a rope. I placed it around my waist and he hauled me up the smooth side of the boat. Onlookers appeared and leant over the railings, pointing.

On reaching the very railings I'd earlier somersaulted over, I grabbed hold of my Dad. 'Am I glad to see you,'

I said. He hugged me back and someone said 'Ahhh,' softly, while another clapped.

'I ran up on deck after I went to your cabin and noticed your empty hammock. Through binoculars, I could see your sawfish flying backwards through the air and assumed you must have caused that. So, motor on full speed, I steered Sea-Ya in your direction.' He started lifting me over the railings when a look of horror appeared on his face. He roughly pushed me to one side as the sawfish rammed its cutting nose into a gap in the railings, just missing my side. It jiggered and waggled to either chop up the railings or free itself. Dad and I helped the beast to make up its mind. I thumped it and Dad pushed its head. Together we released the creature. It fell backwards for the second time this morning and (later), Dad agreed with me – it had a sad face!

As I dried myself on deck, I looked up to see what was making loud and familiar off-tune squawking. A short distance away from the yacht, a lone seagull chased a sawfish that danced on the surface of the water with a blue flip-flop on the end of its nose.

'That was my latest escape adventure,' I said to the silent audience. I gave a small bow then I raised my souvenir elastic waistband above my head. 'This saved me.' No one clapped. The silence was baffling and unexpected. Maybe they hadn't liked my story. Or had I been transported to another planet like Earth, only the language was different.

At the side of the stage, Chloe smiled, waved and gave a thumbs up. A baby at the back wailed. Someone dropped a plastic cup and the sound echoed through the hall as it bounced on the wooden floor five times. A square-shaped figure near the back of the hall got up and walked down the central passage towards the stage. My eyes, blurry from the lights, couldn't make out who . . . He clapped. Others joined in and soon everyone was clapping. And the man I knew stood beside me and said, 'What a smashing fishy tale.'

He turned to the audience and shouted over the clapping, 'Give it up for Deni – my amazing daughter!' The audience came alive and clapped harder. I held my elastic waistband up and stretched it out above my head. Then I tore up my notes and flipped the pile up and over us. 'You did make it here after all!' I said, and kissed him on the cheek.

Chloe dashed over. 'I think they liked your story.'

I knew at that point it was attention, attention, attention that motivated me. I wanted more, more, more!

The clapping stopped as the headteacher clambered onto the stage with a look of anger bursting out all over her face. She took hold of the microphone. 'Ladies and gentlemen, boys and girls. I have decided to stop this extravaganza event because an unidentified boy has set off a fire extinguisher in the male staff toilet.' Chloe was quite relieved to discover that she wouldn't be reading her story after all.

She whispered to me, 'I felt sick when your story came to its end. I was ready to run away and hide in a wheely bin. '

'Black, green or brown?'

10 A Prisoner in Kaarmastan

(Story by Tony Tutting,
as told on the boat.)

Kaarmastan

You won't find it on a map, but go and see
This place, far away across the sea.
Explore the unknown, giant mountains so white.
It's near India – just to the right.

No posh hotels or massive meals,
No buses, trains or cars with wheels.
Where life is short and cruel and rough
And the goat-herds here are mean and tough.

Kingdom of battles, poor Kaarmastan.
Where ten goats are born to every man.
A visit here, will you attend?
And walk my path to our journey's end.

Searching for adventure, my journey started with an exhausting plod up and up and up into the high peaks of Kaarmastan. My loud whistling attracted interest from a crew of local shepherds who appeared magically from behind a scattering of large boulders. The grim-looking bunch surrounded me. They didn't seem to be keen to show me the museums and beauty spots of Kaarmastan. Instead, they closed in around me and, without warning, beat me with sticks. Holding out my hands to protect myself proved a waste of effort and they received a good clobbering. The pain was unbearable.

A skinny guy with a rifle looked as though he was the gang's chief. I held out my wristwatch to him and said, 'Please take it and stop hitting me.' But he laughed, grabbed the watch and whacked me on the head with his rifle butt. I fell unconscious to the dirt.

I woke with a throbbing headache in an almost pitch black room lying face down on mouldy straw. It smelled like a sewer. The walls, dripping with condensation, were made of huge lumps of rock. A feeble trickle of daylight crept in through a tiny opening high up near a corrugated iron roof.

It was painful moving, but I forced myself to sit up, resting my back against the cool rock wall. I heard a scraping sound and a scrawny rat scuttled across the floor. It sniffed me as it passed. At least I had some company.

'Pig-dog,' someone said, and it startled me. I wasn't alone. My eyes could not focus well enough to see the mystery speaker. 'Pig-dog tourist. You must pay monies.'

What did he mean? "You pay monies."

I faced the direction of the voice and prepared to speak when a kick to my ribs came out of the darkness. It knocked me flat to the floor in agony. The hospitality of the local area did not seem as generous as I had expected. ("Warm and friendly people," the guidebook said.)

I spoke to the boot. 'Your English is very welcoming, which is more than I can say for the kicks. What exactly do you want?' Another kick followed from the invisible boot. 'Oh, not again. Please.'

'I want monies – dollar, pound, euro, shilling. I don't care which. No credit card or Tesco vouchers. Pay me now or stay in my lovely hotel for ever,' said the voice in the darkness.

Lifting my head up a short way, I squinted to see who had been talking to me and kicking me. Very slowly, the figure of a man appeared as my eyes adjusted to the poor quality of light.

My tormentor sat on a three-legged stool holding a rusty Victorian rifle, left over from some long-forgotten war, which he pointed threateningly at my face. He wore a typical local costume but on his head there proudly sat a baseball cap with an *I Love NY* badge at the front. Judging by the ragged condition of his clothes, he seemed to be very poor. A grey-black beard dominated his face and he had a fierce look in his left eye. The other eye was covered by a black patch – like a pirate's from the olden days. I mumbled, 'What more do you want from me? You have taken everything.'

'You are mistaken, English,' he said. 'We not take. You give. It's called Tourist Tax and you pay or you will be locked up be in this lovely hotel forever.'

I really appreciated his sense of humour but didn't think much of the room service.

In the stifling heat and dust of the small cell, I coughed. The pain from his kicks growled in my chest.

'You have no right to hold me prisoner. You must let me go. I cannot pay you any money.'

'You refuse to pay! Well, in that case,' the one-eyed stranger growled, 'you stay until you change your mind. I knows well you English persons. I knows Manchester Uniteds, BB and C, Marks with Spencers and Toys of Us. I knows you get one million pounds a week pay.' He stood and tossed my sheepskin jacket on top of me, adding, 'You will need this for the cold nights.'

He clomped out, slamming a thick wooden door loudly after him, locking me inside. I heard the keys leave the lock and his footsteps echo into silence.

Raising myself as best I could I dragged my sore body to the nearest wall where I rested my back against the cool rock for the second time. When I'd recovered my breath, I reached into the pocket of my sheepskin jacket for a tennis ball. Like Steve McQueen in the war film *The Great Escape*, I bounced the ball off the floor and on to the opposite wall. The steady rhythm of the bouncing ball stopped me thinking about my sore body and how careless I had been in coming to Kaarmastan without a proper guide to keep me out of trouble.

My game lasted five or so minutes until I grew tired and weak. I tossed the ball away into the dark corner on my left and got quite a shock in return.

'Ouch, that hurt,' someone said, and it didn't sound like the bullying jailer.

Opening my eyes wide, I noticed for the first time something alive – a child. It squatted at the base of the wall, with chains on its wrists binding the unfortunate creature to the wall. Astounded, I glared open-mouthed at the prisoner – more a skeleton than a person. A pile of scaffolding rather than a building.

'Who *are* you?' I asked, hoping we could speak English.

A rough voice, sounding as though it hadn't been used for ages, croaked, 'Greetings and welcome to you stranger. Allow me to present myself. I am Princess Kaarma, the true ruler of Kaarmastan. Sadly, I have been robbed of my kingdom by my evil younger brother who, once I escape, will pay for his greed. I am glad to be of your acquaintance.'

I was taken aback at the prisoner being a woman and impressed by her lengthy greeting and the old-fashioned, educated tone of her crackly voice. My eyes, now more used to the gloomy conditions within the cell, allowed me to see a pathetic and mistreated person. Starvation had turned her into a bag of bones thinly covered by worn threads of what were once a shirt and pants.

'Princess Kaarma . . . of Kaarmastan,' I repeated. 'You speak good English.'

'I went to school in Southend.' I've been a prisoner in this dungeon for two years. Plenty of time to plan an escape! But, as you can see I am a little tied up,' and she rattled her rusty chains. With a hint of laughter in her voice, I could tell she delighted in my company. 'I am here as a guest of my evil brother who has taken my throne and crowned himself king – totally against the law and the wishes of my people.'

'I'm sorry to hear that. And you've been here for two years! What a miserable existence.'

'It is painful and very bad for my health. The food is worse than pig's swill. My hair is unwashed and if I could grow a beard, it would have reached to my feet. I've really missed watching "Eastenders" on TV. It reminds me of my time in Southend.'

'I couldn't imagine two years in this rotten hole, but you mentioned escaping.'

'Yes. I need the key to the locks to release myself from the wall, but alas, I cannot turn the key as both my hands are in irons.' She managed another weak rattle of the chains above her shoulders. Her thin, bony and bruised wrists had been stretched in their chains. Pussy sores swelled up on every part of her body. That sad princess desperately needed a doctor. I had to help her escape in any way I could.

She continued. 'The guard, Tonsil, is very stupid and forgetful. He can easily be tricked. He is so stupid he once locked his rifle in this cell with me for a whole day! Unfortunately, as you can imagine, I could do nothing on that occasion to free myself.'

'Well, *my* hands are free. Should I try to overpower Tonsil when he next comes in?'

'Not exactly. I will tell you how you can be of assistance for I have thought deeply about freedom and getting back the throne of my country. Luckily for us, you have been blessed with our means of escaping from this hell.'

The brown rat scuttled back across the floor, a piece of straw in its mouth.

'Are you sure *I* have the means to escape?' I asked, puzzled by her suggestion. 'Tonsil has taken everything I own except my tennis ball.'

'You do have the means. And if we are successful, you can expect to a reward at least as valuable as your stolen luggage!'

I sat up, feeling a bit more positive now I had some hope of escaping. 'Then tell me the plan, your highness.'

Princess Kaarma glanced here and there as though checking for spies or guards that might be listening. 'You haven't seen the notice, have you?' she enquired.

'What notice?'

'Over there.' The princess nodded towards the opposite wall.

Sure enough, a notice of some sort hung on the wall. I struggled to read the words in the semi-darkness. Its worn and chipped lettering, hand-painted on a piece of rotting wood, presented a bit of a challenge. I moved closer to the notice for a clearer view. 'No . . . ani . . . '

'No animals allowed,' croaked the princess, impatiently. 'That's what it says. This glorious rule will save us.'

'I don't understand. Do you want me to hit Tonsil with the sign?'

'Not at all. I will make it clear. But first, tell me, what is *your* name?'

'Anthony Tutting, but please call me Tony.'

'Gracious to meet you, Tony Tutting. I'm sorry our get-together is not in more comfortable surroundings.'

To my fellow captive I crawled and shook her right hand in its chains. It was like holding a bunch of cold clothes pegs. 'Pleased to meet you, princess.'

'An unusual name, Tutting. My dead father, who was the king, always tutted – especially at me. He was probably a dolphin in another lifetime.'

The poor princess's face resembled a mouldy apple covered in bruises and oily lumps. Dirt and dust had found its way into every wrinkle and on to every strand of her hair. Her bare shoulders had no muscle and her ribs were stone steps. She smelled like one of those toilets you find in underpasses. Frightening of all were the deep black ponds of darkness in her eyes where there should have been colour and celebration.

'Now tell me, princess, how are we going to escape?'

'I told you Tonsil the guard is very stupid, of that there is no doubt. Most of these mountain men have not had much schooling and they can be as idiotic as a goat. Tonsil's crazy sense of humour centres on his sign, "NO ANIMALS ALLOWED." He refers to us as animals. You are *Pig-Dog* and I am *Donkey Head.* The sign is his silly joke.'

It hadn't made me laugh but I nodded to show I'd understood.

'Tonsil often tells me, "You are Donkey Head and *I* am the prince." So now it's his turn to be the victim.'

'And how can that sign be useful to us?'

'It's straightforward my friend. You must dress up as a sheep.'

I looked at Kaarma hoping she was joking. 'You mean turn my jacket inside out so the fleece imitates a real sheep?'

'That's right, my friend. And add a straw-filled sock for the face. In this dim light Tonsil will think you are a real sheep. He will be falling for our trick, how you say? Hook, line and stinker.'

'It's *sinker*. Hook, line and *sinker* – like in fishing.'

'Tonsil will be stunned by your sudden appearance as a sheep and, while he puzzles out what to do, you will over-power him and steal his rifle and keys. That is how we will escape. As soon as I saw your jacket I knew the plan could be launched.'

I understood the plan. I stuffed straw into my woollen sock, tied a shoelace to it and attached it to my head. 'What time will Tonsil come back?'

'He is unpredictable and cannot tell the time. Meals can be at any time that he feels like cooking, day or night, and it's meal-time that you must be ready to strike him down.'

Both of us waited for Tonsil's arrival and, dressed as a sheep, I crouched in front of the door. But the longer we waited the more impatient I became. I couldn't breathe properly through my stuffed sock and my kneecaps began to ache. Our plan could fail if I were to give up early because of exhaustion.

Glancing over to Kaarma, I realised how much and how long she'd suffered. I had to stay awake and ready, for her sake.

Just when I really felt like giving up altogether, Tonsil put his key in the cell door lock.

'Get ready, Tony. Here he comes.'

Tonsil turned the key, opened the door and picked up the plates of mouldy food from the shelf outside the cell. As expected, he entered the room with each hand holding a plate and his ancient rifle slung over a shoulder.

Tonsil looked down at me and, with some shock in his voice, he asked, 'What do you tink you are doing? Can't you see the sign? NO ANIMALS ALLOWED.'

Tony the sheep jumped up, rammed the old goat Tonsil in the stomach and sent him reeling backwards. His head banged against the door frame, knocking him out. He lay completely still on his back – the plates of food gripped firmly in his hands.

Deep in Tonsil's pockets, I searched and found the keys to Kaarma's hand locks. With caring gentleness, I released her from the wall. Her arms were so sore and weak that she couldn't use them at all. I helped her to stand but she couldn't walk. I scooped her up and carried her like a baby out of the pit of hell.

We left Tonsil with the rats nibbling at his plates of food.

'Free at last!' exclaimed the joyful princess as we left the cell. However, as she entered daylight for the first time in over seven hundred days, she cried out, 'I can no longer see! I'm blind. We waited at the exit until princess Kaarma gradually got used to the brightness of the daylight. 'We are free, Tony Tutting, free! You rescued me. One day I will pay you back.'

'I just thought of something. Do excuse me for a moment,' I said, and I dashed back to the cell. Using the cell key, I scraped the "NO" from the sign and locked Tonsil in with his new furry friends.

Princess Kaarma grew healthier over the next few months and gradually got back her strength, had her hair styled and watched dozens of episodes of "Eastenders" on TV Kaarmastan.

Her evil brother sent a thousand soldiers to look for Kaarma. He offered a fifty-five-year-old Morris Minor car (without doors and with only three wheels) as a reward for finding her, dead or alive. She hid in a doctor's house while she recovered and I stayed by her bedside.

Six months after that, with a small army of supporters, princess Kaarma took back her tiny country from her evil brother and she was crowned Queen Kaarma the 17th of Kaarmastan.

For my efforts, she rewarded me with twenty of her best donkeys. Needless-to-say, I had to leave all my new wealth behind in order to fly back to England with a one bag allowance of fifteen kilos! No room for donkeys. (No animals allowed.)

In London, at airport security, I set off the metal detector alarm. The customs officer asked, 'Are you carrying anything metal?' I put my hand in my pocket and discovered Tonsil's rusty cell key.

11 Solid Friends, Solid Enemies

Chloe and I sat halfway up my stairs, waiting for Dad to get ready. I nudged her lightly in the ribs. 'We're going to the hospital, and we're not even sick!'

'I don't think I've been to hospital since I was born,' she said.

'No x-rays, no ambulance, no bandages, no injections. Just loads of talk, talk, talk.'

Chloe's mum, Lucy, worked as a nurse in the births section of the Norfolk Hospital, and she had made arrangements for me to be interviewed on Radio GetWell, ("The radio station with the groovy medicine.") They didn't just play songs. They interviewed writers, marathon runners, soldiers back from the Middle East, that sort of person. Well, *I* was that sort of person – a bit of a celebrity.

Being on the hospital radio will give me publicity if ever I decided to write my life story. But a lot more stuff will need to happen to me before I have enough to put in a book. I might have a chapter about how Chloe and I became friends at Dog Lane Primary.

'Do you remember making me cry on our first day at school?' I asked Chloe. 'I'd made a wooden brick castle which you demolished by crashing an enormous red train into it.'

'You called me "a lousy driver" and I said you should've lowered your ramp.'

'And I told you, "It's not a ramp, silly. It's a drawbridge."'

'And I said, "You're the silly one, Deli Tum-ting. How can a bridge draw?" We laughed for ages.'

'Solid friends, right at that moment. It was the laughter that clinched it. In every class we've been in we've always sat together, laughed together, cried together and copied each other whenever we got stuck.'

Chloe developed a talent for maths. She did all my multiplication and division and I helped her with writing. I wrote her first story – *Wot I does did on holadey.*

We followed a tradition of giving each other silly, useless things as birthday presents. This year I gave her a second-hand guidebook; *Pylons and Lampposts of Great Britain and Northern Ireland (in Welsh)*. She hated it. On my thirteenth, she gave me a *National Union of Mineworkers* ashtray. I kept Maltesers in it.

Watchett, also in our class from day one, gave us the nickname "The Brown Plops" after our similarly coloured hair. When his mum married for the second time, Tom Watchett became Dirk Watchett (named after his mum's favourite film actor). I preferred Tom. Back then, he often smiled at me across the room, sharpened my pencils until they were half size and ate my break-time snacks. Tom Watchett turned into a different boy when he got a new step-dad. He dumped his friendly smile and became a pest.

'All we ever seemed to do in those days was laugh,' Chloe said. 'But, what did we laugh about?'

'Everything made us laugh. Remember that dinner lady, Mrs Stormy? She had five children in the school at the same time and all named after the weather! Year 6 had Wayne. Year 5 had Gale. Year 4 had identical twins, Misty and Summer, while little Sonny brightened up Year 3.'

'Crazy, eh?'

'We were nearly expelled once when we upset Mr Strong (nickname 'Mustard').'

'Oh, don't remind me, Deni.'

Mustard had asked for helpers to act as parents in his Evacuation Day drama. (During World War Two, children were sent to live the countryside when the towns and cities were bombed.) Chloe and I volunteered to play the part of parents and Mustard asked us to dress in 1940s style. We raided the drama costume cupboard, opened the door, and stinky old clothes tumbled to the floor. Costumes of past performances formed a heap in front of us; two Norman helmets, a Roman sword, loads of brown Tudor waistcoats, Victorian bonnets and a class-load of sheets for dressing up as ancient Greeks. We rummaged through the pile and found the perfect items for 1940 – as worn by comedy film clowns Laurel and Hardy; bowler hats, shirts, ties and pants.

When Evacuation Day came we assembled in the hall to perform our drama in front of the whole school. Some of the younger kids were sniggering at my painted-on moustache.

All went quiet as Mustard entered the hall dressed as a soldier and he spoke loudly, as I imagined all soldiers did. "Good morning, children. Today you travel by train to the countryside where you will be safe."

He saw Chloe and I. "Crikey, Tutting and Clarke. What the hell are you playing at?"

"You said dress 1940s style . . ."

"Get out of this assembly, now." He stamped a metal-rimmed brown boot forcefully on the wooden floor and pointed to the exit. We acted as Laurel and Hardy in their old black and white films. I said aloud to Chloe (Laurel), "That's another fine mess you've gotten me into."

(Back to the stairs)
Sitting for so long made me restless and I bumped down two steps shouting, 'Can you hurry, Dad? We'll be late.'

At least he had made an effort to be with me at the hospital. I admired him for showing some interest in my life.

'You two ready yet?' he asked, thumping down the stairs and buttoning up his jacket. He stopped behind me, put his hands over my eyes and asked, 'Guess who?' The smell of his Brut aftershave frightened my nose.

'We've been waiting for you, Mr Tutting,' Chloe said, tapping her watch with a finger. She had a cheeky attitude towards Dad, which he accepted.

'C'mon girls, hospital appointments are a serious business. We can't be late and parking there is a nightmare. Radio waits for no man.'

'Or girl,' I added.

We clambered down the stairs to the hallway. Chloe jumped the last three steps. If I'd done that I'd have been told off. Somehow she got away with naughty things. That's one reason I liked her.

'Get in the car, girls. It's open,' Dad ordered, locking the front door. But as soon as we got to the stony drive and saw our car we froze. Dad joined us and asked, 'What's the holdup? You look like you've seen a . . . What the blazes?' That's how he swore when he was shocked. Dad tried to avoid swearing, unless a crisis occurred or he just couldn't help himself.

Chloe stared wide-eyed at the car. 'It's not grey anymore, Mr Tutting.'

'It's turned white yet it hasn't snowed,' I added.

With both hands open, Dad crept towards his beloved Ford Mondeo, which *was* grey but . . . 'My poor motor. It's been covered in white words . . . from one of those cake icing pens! And the icing's hardened.'

Walking slowly around the mostly white car, we read out some of the iced words. *"Lies, all lies. She's in a dream world. Don't believe her. Famous? – Never. She couldn't escape from a dead snail."*

Very noticeable on the bonnet, right in front of the driver's view, the often-repeated insult *"BROWN PLOPS,"* lay scribbled in the thickest and largest capital letters which attracted the eye like graffiti on the side of a bridge.

'Curse this doodler. It's outrageous!' said Dad. He glared at us and asked, 'What's this all about?' We shrugged our shoulders.

I said, 'It's just sugar. It'll wash off. No damage done.'

Dad turned away. Chloe and I looked at each other and nodded. We knew who did it.

‘We can’t delay any longer. Get in girls. I’ll have to drive it as it is.’ He flicked a blob of icing from a wing mirror.

All the way to the hospital, people pointed and chuckled. Some might have thought the Lord Major’s procession had started early. Passing car drivers hooted and a policeman in a patrol car lowered his widow and shouted, ‘Have you just married?’

12 Polar Bears! Who Cares?

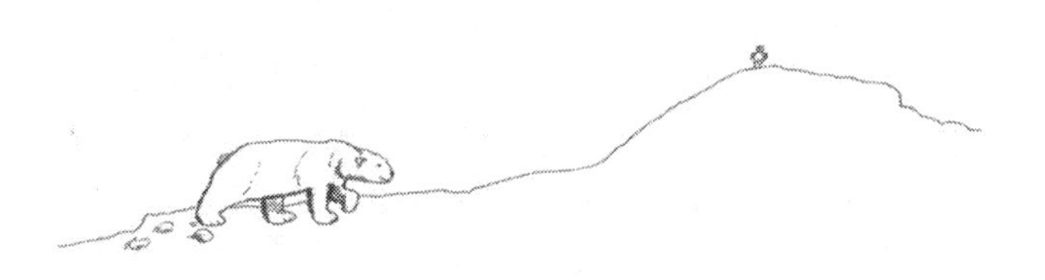

Arriving at the hospital in good time, we hurried from our wedding cake car to the Radio GetWell studio on the fourth floor of the hospital. A posh-voiced woman, dressed in a smart tartan suit, met us as we entered and introduced herself as Gwendolyn. She pinned name badges on each of us and showed us into the recording studio – a small room bursting with electronic gadgets, computers, flickering lights and a lengthy table with rows and rows of knobs and switches. I wanted to run my hands over those switches and flip them on and off to see what would happen.

Barry Bowman stood up when he saw us standing at the door. His head nearly touched the ceiling. A wispy black goatee beard on a paper-white face gave a ghostly impression. He lowered his headphones to his neck, shook our hands and beamed, 'Welcome everyone.' I bounced up and down and clapped, as I tended to do when excited. Chloe was excited too. She'd spotted a dish of M&Ms and kept sneaking the orange ones when Barry wasn't looking.

'I'll want only Deni to speak in the interview. Dad and Chloe – you may sit and watch as long as you don't join in, okay? Now, where's my blue notepad?' He rummaged around his paper-littered desk tossing odd sheets into the air or on to the floor. 'Here it is. "Deni Tutting – trip to the Arctic." It's got all my notes and questions in the right order. Don't want to get muddled now do we? Not with all those wards full of sick people and doctors and nurses and porters and visitors listening to us.'

My interview, due to start at two minutes past three, immediately after the hospital news headlines, would be "live" – so no umming and ahhing. A massive clock on the wall behind me slowly chugged towards broadcasting time. I glanced over at Chloe. She stuck out her orange stained tongue and pointed to a corner of the studio where a lonely old Pudsey Bear sat on a dusty filing cabinet. A bandana covered both of his eyes and someone had placed a cigarette in his mouth.

'Here we go then. Silence, please,' Barry ordered, as he flicked a switch. A red light came on and lit up the words ON AIR in a box next to the clock. Barry spoke into his microphone, 'Welcome patients, staff and public, to *Meet My Guest*.' A short piano tune followed.

'On the show today my very special guest this week is thirteen-year-old traveller and local gal, Deni Tutting, who's glad to be alive following a near-death encounter with a polar bear! Yes, it's true folks. You might think you've had a close encounter with your doctor on the operating table, but could you possibly imagine the sheer excitement and danger in meeting the world's biggest bear – and getting away alive? Well, stay tuned because all will be revealed. And remember; don't spread germs – spread happiness.' Again, the little tune played.

I was bursting to start the interview and shuffled about on my canvas chair, which had large letters on the back saying, GUEST. Perhaps it should have said,

NERVOUS WRECK or LET ME OUT OF HERE. It felt sort of weird speaking to an invisible audience. Gwendolyn said there would be over one thousand listeners, in beds, in wards, on trolleys, in corridors, in waiting rooms. All listening to me.

Barry faced me across a wide table. 'OK Deni, ready or not.'

For no reason, my tongue popped out.

A mystery voice counted, '5,4,3,2,1, on air.'

'Deni, hello. It's a pleasure to have you on *Meet My Guest.*'

'Hello, Barry,' I replied, still shifting about in my special chair.

'A brave girl who's a bit nervous, but you've brought along your best mate Chloe and Tony your old man. So let's get to the bottom of this story, Deni. What were you doing in the North Pole in the first place? It's not the kind of holiday destination most of us would choose to go to, is it?'

'Well, my dad finds special places for films. The Arctic has unusual landscapes that he wanted to collect for the film *Knickerbocker Glory – Quest of the Ice Queen.* That's only a temporary title until they can think of a better one.' I shot a brief glance at Dad and he nodded, smiled and gave me a thumbs up.

'Do you mean to say all scenes in films nowadays are computer-generated?'

'Not all,' I continued. 'Sometimes real locations are used but this time we were collecting films and photos.'

'You're a bit young for being in a hostile environment like the North Pole. Who else went with you?'

'On this particular day there were six others – Dad, two photographers, a guide with a rifle and two guys with equipment on a sledge – food and stuff.'

‘I suppose the gun would come in useful for attacks by pecking penguins.’ We laughed. Barry reminded Dad and Chloe to stay silent.

‘There are no penguins in the North Pole,’ I explained. ‘They’re not allowed out of the South Pole. However, we could have been attacked by all sorts of large animals – polar bears, walruses, seals, caribou. Fortunately, it’s very rare that anyone ever gets . . .’

BANG! The studio door opened forcefully and hit the wall with a crash. In burst a crouching, hooded figure shouting, ‘It’s all made up! She just wants to be famous, that’s all.’

I recognised the voice and I knew the boy.

A yellow uniformed security guard jumped on top of the hooded visitor, wrestling him to the floor. Their arms and legs entwined as Watchett and the security guard fought themselves into a spidery bundle of black and yellow.

With a gloved hand, the guard covered Watchett’s mouth to silence him. After a further tussle, the panting guard grabbed hold of Watchett by his ankles and dragged him back towards the exit. On the way, our hooded friend thumped the door as the last gesture and uttered, ‘Polar bears – who cares?’

Dad got up and closed the door behind them. Chloe thumped a fist into the palm of her other hand and pursed her lips, while Barry remained calm. ‘Sorry about that, folks. A wild animal got loose in the studio! Not a polar bear though!’

He whispered to me, ‘You all right?’ I nodded, though I felt as though I’d been in that fight.

‘Let’s continue the interview. . . So, Deni, what’s it like up north, at the top of the world, Arctic, North Pole – whatever you like to call it?’

I approached the microphone. 'Well, the Arctic isn't land, it's all frozen water. In May, it's daylight all day. There was no real night-time at all. And the cold was like being in a freezer! I breathed on my sunglasses and ice immediately formed on the lens!'

'Isn't nature fascinating?'

'Moving in the deep drifts of snow was difficult. I panted for air because lifting my feet up so high so often just tired me out. I wasn't used to walking in snow boots.

'We'd travelled about a mile from camp. It seemed more like ten miles. We found the towering snow drifts and high ridges that we came to film and the photographers did their job..'

Barry quipped, 'There's a doctor with a white beard who works on Hickling ward. He looks like a polar bear.'

'I suppose that's better than having a polar bear that looks like a doctor!' I said, and we giggled.

'And that's a suitable place to take a break, folks. You're listening to Radio GetWell, Barry Bowman's *Meet My Guest*. We'll be back shortly. Remember to take your pills, and join in all the thrills!' Then he flicked a few switches and we were OFF AIR.

'Right, we'll be playing a few adverts while we have a wee break,' he said. 'It's going well Mr Tutting,' and Dad nodded in agreement, 'apart from our little friend bursting in. Has he got something against Deni?'

I heard Barry's question and my brain wanted to say, "He's a bully," but I answered for Dad with, 'I think he likes me.'

You should have seen Chloe's face when she heard that. Her jaw dropped and her mouth opened like a starving trout's. Her eyebrows danced. She hadn't agreed one bit with my comment.

Of course, Watchett didn't like me. I really don't know why I said he did. I mouthed 'sorry' to Chloe and she gestured back that I might just be a bit mad.

What had I ever done to upset Watchett? I've occasionally called him names – prune face, slug slime, toilet brush. I've heaved the odd brick in his direction. Yet I do know he sort of likes me in a weird way because last February he sent me a Valentine's card two weeks before Valentine's Day. I knew it came from him. I recognised his scrawly handwriting (o like a six).

'You don't mean that, do you? That he really likes you?' Chloe whispered, leaning towards me. I could see in her eyes the answer she wanted.

'No, I didn't mean to say what I said. It sort of slipped out. I hope Barry won't mention it on the radio.'

'Time for the next part, boys and girls,' Barry said. And, with the flick of a switch, we were live on air again. I straightened up in front of the microphone and nodded to Barry to continue.

'Tell us about the polar bears, Deni'.

'Well, the photographers had finished taking photos and films and we set off back to base camp. Our guide spotted a snowstorm coming and arranged us in order. I ended up at the back, tied to the sledge by a four-metre length of rope – like a puppy on a leash.

'We'd only travelled for a few minutes when the snow really whisked up. Flakes the size of apples seemed to appear from nowhere, blocking my vision. I couldn't see the end of the sledge right in front of my face! Walking became impossible when my feet went on strike and refused to move anymore.'

'That sounds dreadful.'

'I stretched my hands out to feel the sledge. It wasn't there. I stretched my hands out to feel the rope. It wasn't there. It remained, however, tied around my waist, but the other end had detached itself from the sledge. I think everybody had moved on without me.'

'You must have been in a right tizz,' said Barry.

'My hated fear of loneliness crept into me. I cried out, "Dad. Where are you?" But the whistling gale and thickness of the snowflakes blocked out my voice.

'Someone in our team had told me that if I got separated I had to stay in that spot until rescued. However, if I stopped I'd soon be covered by snow and turned into a human snowman. If I were able to walk on I'd probably get completely lost. What sort of choice was that? Stay or walk?

'The storm ended as though a door had been closed on it. Dazzling sunshine bounced off the fresh snow and danced at my eyes. Sunglasses on, but I saw no one, heard no one. I tried moving, but the fresh snow had formed a thick suit of armour around my legs and body, locking me in. Only my arms and head were clear of this white prison.'

'How did you break out?' Barry asked.

'Kicking wildly, but it took a while. I climbed to a higher part of the ridge for a better view when I heard a roar that chilled me more than the freezing air could. Polar bears make that roar – I've seen them on TV.

'Why are they feared so much, Deni?'

'Polar bears are carnivores. They can smell a meal over one mile away! If they caught me they'd eat me.

'I noticed a moving black spot below me at the base of the ridge. One moment it was there, the next it was gone, then it returned – a polar bear's nose! I reasoned that if this predator recently emerged from its winter den, then it would be as hungry as a snake chasing a wildebeest. A Deni-kebab for dinner might be on its mind. What else would polar bears have to think about apart from food? There's no laying the table. No washing up to do. No dishwasher to load.

'Then three black spots appeared, one slightly larger than the others. That would be a mother with two cubs. The Three Bears story was becoming real, and I was down to act two parts – Goldilocks *and* the bowl of porridge!

'At the bottom of my ridge, the mummy bear sniffed the air and smelled Haribos and chocolate digestives. She appeared to be the size of a car – with claws for wheels and a humongous mouth where the front number plate goes. She nudged her cubs to run ahead while she followed them up the slope towards me. I had nowhere to hide.'

Barry tapped his watch. 'How did you escape, Deni?'

'I threw a snowball. It missed the target. I may as well be throwing balls of cotton. I had to think of something else – the cubs had already reached halfway up the side of the ridge and were eager to investigate because I was the first living thing they'd ever seen that wasn't a bear.

'I formed a new, larger snowball, like the head of a snowman, patting it, shaping it and rolling it so it grew quickly, picking up the soft snow as it rolled.

'I shoved the snowball over the edge of the ridge towards the furry twins. As it rumbled towards them it grew in size, but its weight soon caused it to stop. I jumped towards it feet first, slammed into it and got it rolling again. Down the ridge it tumbled, crashing into the twins, swallowing them like the sun gobbling up two planets. And it didn't stop there. It kept rolling, flattening mother bear deep into the soft snow.

'I shouted, "Goldilocks wins!" Almost immediately, a loud gunshot made me jump and startled the bears. They scraped with their powerful claws and freed themselves from the heap of snow and slouched away from the boom of the rifle. I don't think the snowball idea would've worked a second time, so you can guess how relieved I was to see Dad and the others.'

'That's been an amazing story, Deni, and I hope we made our patients and staff feel a little better. I know I'd prefer to be tucked up in bed rather than face a wild bear!

'Next week, my guest will be Elizabeth Snitch, lollipop lady at our local primary school. I'll be asking her, "How do you stop all those cars?" So, for now, it's goodbye to our wonderful guest and cheerio listeners till next time. Oh, and I leave you with the joke of the week. What do you call a polar bear with no fur? . . . A polar *bare*!'

'That must be one of our best interviews, Deni. You expressed yourself very clearly.'

'That was really cool,' Chloe said as we bundled into the lift. 'I wish I could have adventures like that. You'll end up in the newspapers or on the internet if you're not careful.'

Outside the building, we were met by a group of boys and girls from my school. They surrounded us, waving notebooks and pens. 'Can I have your signature, Deni?' said a girl I'd seen before but couldn't name.

'Me too,' said another. A few nurses came over to see what was going on.

Dad stepped forward and put his arm around my shoulder. 'What's up, kids?' he asked.

'We heard Deni, like, on the hospital radio while we were visiting our friend in Blickling ward. Thought we'd get a signature.'

Chloe chipped in, 'That sounds cool. Do you want my autograph too?'

'Just Deni's,' said the girl.

‘It’s quite flattering to be asked,’ I said, plucking a waving pen from a random hand. I scribbled my name in a book. Two more books appeared. I autographed those too.

‘That’s enough now,’ said Dad, waving the group aside in a dismissive manner. ‘We’ve had a busy afternoon and want to get home. Thanks for showing an interest.’

I was quite chuffed at having a little fan club. It made me feel like a celebrity. A red carpet would have been nice, with a few photographers, a bit of flag waving and some cheering. I could have dressed up.

‘What a bunch of losers,’ Chloe said, glancing back at the group. ‘I bet they’ll flog those autographs on eBay when you get seriously well-known.’

‘You’re not jealous are you?’

‘Course not. They’re only a bunch of Year 5s.’

On the way to the car park, Dad said, ‘I’m so proud of you, but I think you’ve had too many near misses on our trips – killer bees, sawfish, and polar bears. I might have to think twice about taking you again. It’s becoming too risky.’

‘Yeh, but I’m still here, aren’t I?’ I said, jingling my lucky charm on its chain.

‘So you do believe it’s protecting you.’

‘You said it would. I believed you. This thing has loads of good luck left in it yet.’

13 Who Made the Apple Pie?

My life improved following the hospital radio interview. Dad worked hard at being an extra-special, proper dad. He let me have loads of sleepovers, here and at Chloe's. I've been allowed a day in Norwich to buy shoes and school clothes for my new school term in September, Year 9, and we planned to squeeze in a trip to Africa during the summer holiday. That amounted to a generous eight out of ten to him for effort (and I'm *not* going to cut down the silver birch tree.)

As a reward for being an improving dad, I decided to return his wedding ring. I dug it up from the back garden and tossed it into the middle of a thick bush.

'Dad, come outside, quickly.'

'What is it, Deni? I'm cooking supper,' he groaned from the back door, scraping the burnt bits from some unidentifiable solid object. He saw me beckoning and stepped outside wearing his *I Love Frying* apron. He had an annoyed but curious expression on his face.

'Come and see what I see in that bush.' I pointed to the thick lilac shrub below the kitchen window. Mum planted it when I had my sixth birthday.

He came and stooped over the bush, pushing aside its branches and perfumed flowers with the long knife in his hand. 'Gordon Bennett! My lost wedding ring! You found it, Deni, my little star!' He stepped nearer the bush. Stretching deep into its centre, he reached out for the ring and grasped it firmly. It had been over a year since he last saw it.

How quickly an adult's mood can change. He appeared instantly happier. It was pleasing to see him smile as he rubbed the dirt from the ring. 'How come, if it hasn't been in the ground all these months, it's covered in sticky mud?'

I shrugged my shoulders, 'I dunno.'

Dad rinsed the ring under the garden tap, wiped it on his apron and placed it on his wedding ring finger. Admiring his hand, turning it back and forth, he smiled again. 'It's where it belongs. I'm complete at last.' He sat down on the grass, gazed up at the sky, and cried.

Returning the ring was a relief for me. For so long I'd thought about what a mean act it had been to hide it and keep it hidden. Every time I went to the back garden, or even just glanced at it, I thought of the ring. It burnt a circle on my brain.

I wasn't perfect, nor was Dad. But, we showed signs of improvement. However, one activity remained a failure – his cooking. A score of minus two out of ten was as generous as I could be.

About a week ago, he persuaded me to cook a sausage, bacon and egg breakfast – a task I did not want to take on permanently. So I deliberately copied him and burnt the food. 'Obviously, poor cooking ability runs in the family,' he said, as the grill pan went up in flames. He hasn't asked me to cook again.

We invented names for his regular disasters. Chicken pie became farmhouse brick. Pizza was known as the iron frisbee, and boiled egg was golf ball.

Recovering his wedding ring kept Dad in good spirits for days. I watched what I wanted on TV *before* seven pm. My own biscuit tin was kept topped up and we had an Italian pizza in Miglio's floating restaurant. I would say that lots of love for my dad was coming back, and not just because he gave me things. I felt kindness and caring from him and found that his good spirits somehow seeped into me.

Oh, he was happy all right, but for another reason.

To her surprise, Chloe received an invitation from Dad to "a sit-down afternoon tea." That wasn't a regular event in our house but something Dad dreamt up. He said it was "a special occasion" and he expected me to act appropriately (no eating with my fingers/say please/put the milk in the cup first/don't pick your nose).

That afternoon, while Dad prepared the special tea, Chloe and I crashed out in the sitting room with a laptop deciding which shops to visit on our coming trip to the city. I liked *Pants Pants* in the mall, while she preferred *Head Shoulders Hips n Toes* opposite the old market. We'd planned for lunch near the castle, at The Scoffing Place.

Through the open sitting room doorway, a most tempting smell of freshly baked pastry, not burnt, began to waft into the room. The wonderful aroma grabbed hold of my nose and tickled my taste buds. What magic had Dad worked to produce such a temptation?

'Can you smell that deliciousness drifting in from the kitchen?' I asked Chloe. 'There hasn't been such delight since Mum left. What can it be? Let's go and spy.'

With a concern that our giggling might give us away,

we sneaked across the hallway and peered into the kitchen. The table had been transformed. On a neat, light blue tablecloth, China teacups and plates were invitingly arranged. Proper napkins, not sheets of kitchen roll, had been folded and stood upright on each plate. But the main attraction dominated the middle of the display – a massive fruity pie, newly baked and perfectly browned all over. Thick pastry leaves decorated the top and I could smell the exotic aroma of cinnamon. 'That can't be Dad's pie,' I said. 'He doesn't do toast never mind a huge pie!'

'He got it from Morrison's. I've seen them there,' said Chloe.

Dad heard us. 'Come in girls. You're dead on time.'

Chloe and I examined the pie close up. It had obviously been very carefully made, but it couldn't have come from Morrison's because in its centre it had C and D in large pastry letters. When Chloe saw the pie, she took in a swift gulp of air and put her hand over her mouth. Now, what had she spotted?

Dad smiled and almost danced around the table adjusting cups and straightening cutlery. 'Girls, that's a homemade, freshly baked apple pie. Isn't it magnificent? It should be in a museum for pies!'

Our kitchen had not seen such a delight since mum left. Even the oven was crying.

Dad placed Chloe opposite me at the table, and he sat in between us. She had something to say but couldn't or wouldn't say it. Instead, she insisted on annoying me with kicking under the table. She made silly faces whenever Dad faced the other way. What did she want?

The initials interested me. 'Does the C and D stand for Chloe and . . . ?'

‘. . . and Deni. A thoughtful idea, don’t you think?’ Dad asked.

He stood back and admired his table. The boiling kettle whistled on the cooker.

I could only guess that Gran had made the pie. It presented a puzzle to be solved. Furthermore, with the table set for four, who else had been invited?

‘Who else is coming?’ I asked, just as the doorbell rang.

‘That’ll be her now. I’ll get it,’ said Dad as he dashed to answer the door.

I heard the front door open, two “hellos,” and what sounded like a kiss on a cheek. It didn’t sound like Gran though.

Chloe whispered, ‘I know who made the pie. It was my . . .’

Lucy entered the kitchen with a, ‘Hi, girls.’

‘. . . mum!’

Throughout tea, Chloe and I hardly spoke, whereas Lucy and Dad had so much to say they almost forgot to dish up the magnificent apple pie. It was a relief to be dismissed from the table. We ran upstairs and I slammed my bedroom door shut. Garlic Breath was not pleased to see us.

‘Couldn’t you have asked your mum if she’s going out with my dad?’

‘Why me? You could’ve asked your dad the same question.’

‘We’ve missed a good chance to find out. But the clues are becoming clearer. First, they meet at the café, then he gives her a painting, then she makes a to-die-for pie, then she comes round for tea. Is that “going out” or not?’

‘There’s one puzzle still buzzing in my mind. Is my mum the mystery woman that Watchett saw in the café?’

'We'll just have to ask him. Have you got a photo of your mum?'

'Got loads on my mobile.'

'On Monday we'll ask him. I think we need to know.'

Chloe stood, took a deep breath, and said, 'Listen, pie face, I'm gonna clear off now, if that's OK. See you around.' And passing through the doorway waving she added, 'Now that I'm leaving, Garlic Breath seems a lot happier.'

Miss Dobson was on playground duty when Chloe and I arrived at school Monday morning. That would be good for us as Dobson didn't mind a bit of rough play, which was what we had in mind for Dirk Watchett. Some teachers would give a detention if you just *thought* about breaking the rules. Dobson was easy-going.

We watched the area outside the boys' toilets where Watchett and his friends met. But the bell rang and he hadn't appeared.

He was, however, present in class. So, at break time, we again waited near his HQ. We didn't have long to wait. His distinctive laughter, like that of a hyena crossed with a chimpanzee, told us he'd arrived. It dominated that end of the playground. 'Let's go get him. Got your mobile?'

'Yeh. Loading a picture of mum.'

Watchett saw us too late for him to run. I grabbed hold of the front of his jacket and pinned him to the wall.

Chloe thrust her phone into his face. 'Look at the photo,' I demanded. 'Is this the woman you saw with my dad in the café?'

'Are you still going on about that? I could report you for assault.'

I pushed him against the wall again. 'Well, *is* she?'

Watchett moved his head back slightly to focus on the photo. He showed no reaction at seeing a picture of Lucy in her back garden with sausages on a barbecue. 'Hard to tell. I only saw her from the side, from right across the road.'

'We need to know, Watchett,' I said. 'You're gonna give me the truth.'

'You can't hurt me. I've got what you're gonna get, up here.' He tapped his head.

'And I've got what you're gonna get right here, (I showed him my fist). And if I don't get what I'm gonna get then you'll get what you're gonna get.'

Chloe said, 'Do you think you two could speak English otherwise you'll both get what you're gonna get?'

She took over my hold of the jacket and showed Watchett the second image, a side view. 'Listen pizza face. We need a definite yes or no. Is this the woman?'

A dozen or so kids, mainly boys, had gathered around to see the action.

We flinched on hearing a booming voice shout, 'Let go of that boy, Clarke!' Chloe immediately dropped her grip on Watchett. She turned and faced the deputy head, Mr Ryce (nickname 'Basmati'). He took her mobile and asked Watchett if he was all right. 'This is a no bullying school,' Basmati reminded Chloe. 'Call into my office after school, Clarke, for an incident report to your parents. Mobiles are not allowed. I'm sure you're aware,' he said, grabbing the phone just as the bell ended the break.

We still had no answer to our question. I felt sorry for Chloe, caught just as she took hold of Watchett. I felt responsible for that.

Halfway through maths, Chloe doing my long multiplications, a tiny folded note landed on my desk. Fortunately, Miss Fuddy, who detested note passing, was distracted at the whiteboard searching for pens that had gone astray. The note read; "The woman in the café *is* Lucy Clarke. I'd recognise her anywhere."

Looking at the handwriting, with the o more like a 6, there was no doubt the note came from Watchett. Maybe he felt guilty for Chloe ending up with a report.

I didn't show the note to Chloe till lunchtime, as all she could think about was Basmati's report to her mum and how annoyed her mum would be at seeing it.

Dead on three-thirty, a nervous, sweaty Chloe knocked on the deputy's door in admin. 'Enter,' came the familiar voice from within.

'I'll wait for you,' I murmured, as she stepped sheepishly into the room. Then I sat outside Basmati's office in the "naughty chair," feeling guilty whenever anybody walked past and gave me a stare.

Five minutes later, Chloe emerged from Basmati's office, not only smiling but waving her mobile. 'You got off without a report! Did you bribe Basmati with a year's supply of digestives?'

'He knows what Watchett's like and he saw I didn't hit him. Basmati went easy on me.'

'Boil in the bag, or what? Let's get home and see if my dad and your mum are engaged yet.'

'We could end up as sisters!'

'Yeh, and you'll be Chloe Tutting!'

'We'll be the Tutting twins! Scourge of Year 9.'

We skipped across the almost empty playground, arm-in-arm and singing; 'Here come the twins! Here come the twins!'

Lucy

14 A Lion in the Sun

As soon as Dad mentioned a trip to Africa, I fetched my suitcase from the wardrobe and got out the combat clothes I'd worn in Brazil just over a year ago. The jungle and the sweat smells still stuck to the fabrics. I'd hate wearing them again.

I spread the items out on the floor: two scruffy camouflaged tops, two pairs of baggy combat trousers with eight pockets (storage space for Haribos and Hobnobs), a pair of police officer's boots, and worst of all, three pairs of itchy brown socks. Unfortunately, everything still fitted.

Any complaints to Dad about clothing would end up a waste of time. Men just can't understand that girls need to spend hundreds on trendy stuff. 'It's not a fashion show,' he said. 'It's the middle of Africa. No one will notice or care what you look like.'

'*They* might not care. *You* might not care. But *I* care.'

'You'd be out of place wearing your normal summer gear and that's got no protection from the sun. You'll need a hat. Mum left some in our wardrobe. I'll sort one out for you.'

In the part of Africa where we were going, French was the main language spoken. Dad suggested I paid extra attention in my coming French lessons and see if I can pick up any useful phrases. However, (he doesn't know this, so don't tell him), I didn't learn much in any of my French lessons, mainly due to our long-suffering teacher, Madame de la Botte (nickname 'Booty').

She could have been mistaken for a pupil as she was very small. Her face was smooth and tanned. Her large eyes were attractively framed in oval, golden spectacles. The boys loved her perfume. You could smell where she had been by the trail of scent that followed her like a delayed shadow.

And Booty had a crazy habit; no matter what the weather, she always wore a fur coat in class.

We learned nothing because all Booty's skill and knowledge about discipline failed in our classroom. She was totally unable to control us or motivate us. Whenever she shouted or begged for quiet, it just encouraged further silly behaviour; book throwing, pencil flicking, table toppling and near murder. This resulted in a total absence of speaking French. As Booty was so tiny and lightweight, the bigger boys had an easy, nasty habit of lifting her up and standing her on her desk. They did that every lesson, leaving her stranded, unable to get down. All the while she'd cry, 'Put me down boys, please. I beg you. S'il vous plait.'

Also, we discovered she had a dinosaur phobia. When her back was turned, someone would sneak up to her laptop to download images or videos of dinosaurs. On seeing the images, she would burst out crying.

Others brought in toy dinosaurs and placed them around the room. This upset her even more. After every lesson with us, poor Booty left the classroom a nervous wreck (au revoir), and we didn't learn any French (tres bon).

In Africa therefore, I shall have to rely on plain old English.

When the time for our trip came, Dad rummaged through my luggage and removed my mobile. 'It's no good you bringing this. There's no signal where we're going! It's in the middle of nowhere.'

'How will I let Chloe know what's happening? What if I am separated from you, like in the Arctic? Or a snake wraps itself around my leg. What do I do? Send you a postcard?'

'You can always shout!'

'When I fell off the boat I shouted. That proved pointless. I've got my human rights you know. I can take my case to the International Court.'

'Now stop fretting, Deni. We're not going to be separated. I shall watch you this time like a hawk or, as we're in Africa, like a vulture. And there's to be no more escaping from wild animals.'

'Then why take me to a continent packed with wild animals? Isn't that asking for trouble of some sort?'

'You've got your lucky half medal. That'll protect you.'

I looked at him with a fed-up expression. 'Do you honestly think my rescuing hero is just waiting behind some shrivelled shrub or bush ready to spring into action as I scream while falling down a ravine?'

I hated long flights, especially at night. They showed the same film that we saw on the plane to Australia last year (about loads of snakes that got loose on a plane).

On our first day in Africa, we were so tired we just had to rest. Twelve hours I slept, missing two meals.

The following day, Dad said, 'Get your combats on. We're going to the National Park.'

Each piece of clothing needed six shakes to get rid of any hidden spiders or scorpions that may have crawled in during the night. I walloped each sock with a boot, just to be sure.

We travelled to the National Park in an ancient Land Rover with painted black and white stripes resembling a zebra. Our driver, Captain Kwasi Larue, was also the head ranger. He dressed very smartly in a blue uniform. In that oven heat he wore a jacket as well. I couldn't help notice that when he smiled, a huge gap opened up to show his front teeth were missing.

'Have you been in a fight, captain?' I asked.

'No,' he replied, abruptly.

Following us in a similar vehicle were a pair of blue-uniformed wardens. They talked French and smoked non-stop. One was tall, the other short. They carried rifles. When the short one smiled, his gold teeth glistened and he smiled and laughed more than the nervy tall guy.

Dad had explained earlier that the purpose of our trip today was to check out a traditional African village, for a scene in a film called *Race to the Desert in a Double-Decker Bus*. He needed some local people to act in the film and hoped for some volunteers.

Fifteen minutes into the journey, I asked Kwasi, 'Where are we?'

'See that tree over there?'

'Of course.

'Well, we not far from that!'

'Ha, ha, very funny.'

He peeked at me in his rear-view mirror and smiled. Those missing teeth reminded me of the entrance to the tunnel under the English Channel. I had to ask, 'Were you in a car crash?'

'No.'

I got the impression he did not want to discuss his absent teeth, so I turned my attention to the park scenery – dry grass, shrivelled bushes and sun-baked dirt. It smelled like the school playground on a very hot day. We passed a man guiding a scrawny cow with his long stick. That brought back memories of Gran's flood and the cow up a tree. I waved and the man continued his journey, but the cow nodded a "hi" to me.

Kwasi slammed on the brakes. We stopped with a skid on the dry, dusty soil. On a narrow section of the track a massive rhino stood, blocking our way. We didn't have space to pass by the creature as we were squeezed by hedges on either side. It faced us, refusing to budge. It huffed and snorted, nodded its huge head and thrust its horn up and up and up, as if to say, "*Keep back.*" You wouldn't expect it, but the rhino made a noise just like a baby crying.

'Do you want me to get out and shift the rhino, Dad?' (I was joking, of course.)

'You stay exactly where I can see you, miss.'

Inside the Land Rover, I felt the vibrations and powerful energy of that rhino when it stomped the ground.

'This rhino has a name. Can you guess it, Deni?' Kwasi asked.

'Buster . . . I don't know. . . Charles . . . I give up. I don't do guessing games. What is its name?'

'Well, you see his horn? It have a white tip. So we calls him Whitetip. He's famous in the park. I tink he try to be friendly.'

Famous or friendly, the stubborn rhino was in no hurry to move, even when we honked the horn and banged the doors. Kwasi had to reverse the Rover and drive off road to get around the obstruction.

The dirt track ended a mile further on, in a clearing surrounded by shrubs and sad trees. A sign read; *Not to camp over the night. Please to your rubbish take home. By orderings of the head warden.*

Kwasi said, 'We walk now because we not allowed driving any nearer to the village. It's a conservation zone.' (We have a conservation area at school but kids throw rulers and books into the pond.)

Kwasi parked and climbed out to check for lions. He prodded and wacked the shrubs with his long stick as he searched around the edge of the clearing. 'Hey, you two,' he called to his men, waving the stick at them. 'Stop smoking. Look for lions.' I got the impression the men were lazy, or scared of lions.

Dad and I prepared our rucksacks. We'd all been asked to travel light to allow each of us to carry donated gifts for the villagers. I had a box of toothbrushes and Dad carried a pack of T-shirts with *Glastonbury Festival 1987* printed upside down on each one.

'Here's that hat from Mum's collection,' Dad said, throwing it to me screwed up in a ball. I caught it and the hat unfurled.

'That is hideous! A floppy old lady's pink thing with white roses all over.' With the sun sizzling my scalp I had no choice but to put it on. At least by wearing it I didn't have to see it.

Short warden laughed at me. His cigarette dangled from the side of his mouth.

Leaving the cars in the clearing, we trekked for about five minutes. I was quite glad of the rest when it came. Kwasi raised his walking stick and shouted, 'Halt, everyone!'

We had reached the entrance to an old, rickety rope bridge that stretched over a deep gorge with a river below. The bridge had boards to walk on. The whole thing looked as though it could have been made out of recycled materials by a Year 4 class in their design and technology lesson – art straws, cereal boxes, egg cartons and bits of aunties' wool!

'What's the hold-up, Kwasi?' Dad asked, joining me and the captain at the rope bridge.

'Dangerous lion on bridge,' said Kwasi, pointing his walking stick.

I stepped nearer the bridge to see what the fuss was all about. On the far side, a lion dozed in the noon-day sun. Judging by its scruffy, hairy mane it was a male, about the size of a police motorbike. Maybe it had already eaten, was resting, and wouldn't be trouble for us. But it blocked our path, like the rhino earlier, only this time we had no way of going around the animal. I wanted to stroke it.

'We must use this bridge. It's the only river crossing to the village. Can you chase the lion away, Kwasi?' Dad asked.

'No chase. No shoot. Lion protected species.'

His two wardens stood a little way off, whispering to each other and puffing their cigarettes. The tall one couldn't stand still and waved a restless arm in the direction of the lion.

'Maybe we could shake the bridge and wake him up,' I suggested.

'We don't want to upset him, Deni,' said Dad. 'You can't predict what a wild lion will do when faced with five humans in a small space.'

'Lion dangerous. He bite on legs,' said the captain, tapping his boot with the stick.

'I volunteer to go first because I'm the lightest. I'll sneak quietly past him. Maybe he won't wake up.'

Dad tightened his lips and frowned and gave me a *don't you dare* piercing glance. 'I won't let you risk it. It's too dangerous to be anywhere near a lion. What if he woke up as you reached him? I've warned you about getting into fights with wild animals. Anyway, we can always come back tomorrow.'

Kwasi chipped in, 'No tomorrow. We are on elephant patrol.'

'Dad, we've *got* to go *now*. You know I have lots of luck dealing with wild animals. Let me have this chance.'

'It's a chance too far, Deni. As I said back home – you've had too many near misses.'

'I'm wearing my golden charm that *you* said would protect me.'

'You could be eaten, mauled or thrown off the bridge into the river. Stop thinking you're Superwoman and face reality. I love you and don't want to lose you.'

Did all dads over the world say the same things? Could he ever have said this? "Of course you can go and challenge that man-eating lion. Here, use this net and spear – oh, don't forget your sword coated in lion sleeping oil. Good luck, Deni, cheers, see ya later." No, I couldn't picture him saying that.

Dad and the captain started to argue. I heard Dad say, "I've paid you. . . take us across . . . money back . . ."

I heard Kwasi say, “My men do not . . . wait a bit . . . no refund . . .”

Adult talk – I’d had enough of it. I kicked stones over the edge of the gorge into the wild river far below.

Dad and the captain trundled over to the two wardens. There followed a lot of arm waving and head scratching. All four men appeared to be arguing. I waited no longer.

As soon as my hands grabbed the bridge’s rope railings, the monster’s tail twitched. Maybe he felt the vibrations I caused or had picked up my scent, which was a bit strong from heavy sweating. In any event, a cat’s twitching tail meant, *“I don’t like what’s happening.”*

I crept slowly towards the creature, taking great care to watch my feet on the ancient boards that creaked and cracked, causing the lion to twitch an ear. He was very aware of his surroundings and I didn’t want to wake him.

I glanced back at Dad and Kwasi, still arguing. Would they and the wardens ever get across with their heavy boots, noisy rucksacks and dangling rifles?

Sweat dripped off the end of my nose as I eased myself along the boarded walkway, very aware that every step caused the entire bridge to wobble, swing and shake. I kept moving and soon reached the centre of the bridge from where the gushing river and rocks came into full view. I didn’t enjoy the view because I imagined falling through the worm-eaten boards. Then I froze at Dad’s booming voice.

‘Deni Tutting – are you mad?’ he called out. Was he determined to wake the lion by his shouting? I squinted over my shoulder at him, put a finger across my lips and mouthed a ‘shush.’ He ran to the bridge, grabbed hold of the ropes, and was about to step on to the boards when I put up a hand and stopped him. The lion, eyes tightly shut, knocked a fly from his nose with a flip of his tongue.

Nearer and nearer to the beast I crept. On reaching the sleeping beauty, I took a moment to clear my thoughts. There was just enough room to step between his legs and get past, despite him lying across the boards, taking up nearly the whole width of the bridge. However, passing him seemed too much of a risk. I started to turn back to Dad, feeling a bit of a failure because I hadn't found a solution to our furry problem.

The atmosphere was hot and dry. I sweated. Bugs and flying creatures buzzed around my head. A mosquito flew up my nose. It tickled, causing me to sneeze. I froze again and held my breath, fearing I'd woken our snoring friend. I didn't want to be his next meal. But you can't discuss such matters with the king of the jungle. He half-opened his eyes in a sleepy daze, saw me, shook his tail and went back to sleep. In my opinion, he wasn't hungry.

I realised it was the lion's eyes I needed to deal with if we were to get past him. If he can't see, then he might not trouble us. What did I have in my bag that would help? Maybe something reflective; my make-up mirror (Dad called it my shaving mirror).

I carefully reached around to a side pocket in my rucksack, undid the zip little by little and took out my mirror – about the size of a five-pound note. I gripped the rail rope with my right hand and held the mirror in my left, turning it to reflect the sun directly into the monster's closed eyes – eyes that were quite close together. Now, if he opened those eyes, he wouldn't see us creeping past as long as I kept blocking his vision. He'd just see brilliant, blinding light like car headlights! Well, that was the plan – the only plan.

Kwasi and his puffing wardens met Dad at the entrance to the bridge. I beckoned them with my head to come on to the bridge, and I made sure full sunlight covered the beast's eyes.

Kwasi came along the bridge first, panting slightly. He tapped me on the back and whispered, 'When I was fifteen, I drove a motorbike into a wall!' Then he passed behind me carefully, taking care that my reflected sunlight was not disturbed. I had to let go of the rope as he passed me and that caused a bit of a wobble but the lion didn't move.

Dad came next and couldn't resist talking. 'Where did you learn that trick with the mirror?'

'Shush!' I whispered. The lion's tail twitched.

'I'll buy you the biggest ice cream when we get home.'

'Will you keep moving along? You'll wake him.'

The two wardens were next but they hesitated, arguing about who should go first. I waved them towards me, keeping half an eye on my shaky sunbeam. I didn't know how long I could keep the mirror thing going. My raised arm was already tiring.

Eventually, the shorter guy stepped onto the boards, pushed in the back by his mate. His breathing was short and loud. I expected him to cry. He mumbled aloud as he plodded along, stepping too heavily upon the outer edges of the rotting wood, causing the bridge to sway like a hammock.

When Short Guy finally reached me he was dripping with sweat. I thought something bad would happen involving teeth, claws and falling. Yet, despite his noise, the swaying of the bridge and the smell, nothing bad happened. Short Guy tiptoed like a ballet dancer over the lion and reached the safety of land, no problem.

I remained unsure about Tall Guy. He was ultra-slow, taking too long to get going. His progress on the bridge imitated an elderly tortoise on a cold day, struggling with legs that wouldn't bend and a shell too heavy to carry. After having covered only five metres, Tall Guy began flapping both arms and hitting himself. Perhaps a bee buzzed about his head. Then he did the opposite. He froze solid in a bent over pose and peered down through a gap between two planks. His rifle slid off his shoulder and slipped through the gap towards the river, wooden end first. He watched his rifle drop. Down and down and down it fell until it smashed into a large boulder in the river-bed. Immediately, a shot went off with a loud "bang!" Nearby birds flew into the air. The bullet travelled straight upwards, right through Tall Guy's rucksack. He straightened up and ran back towards the start, shouting and cursing, not bothered about where he was treading. At the bridge exit, he glanced up and let out a high-pitched scream. Blocking his way off the bridge was our famous and friendly rhino, Whitetip. Tall Guy flopped to the boards, where he laid face down. He'd had enough.

I heard Dad shouting, 'Deni, run! Lion's waking up!'

The lion stretched his legs and his head and moved out of my dazzling sunbeam. He roared as loud as a stereo on full volume. I staggered backwards and dropped my mirror. It bounced on the board between my feet and then slipped through a gap, like a letter being posted. Down, down it fell, like the rifle, into the raging river. I stood defenceless. My brain told me to run like crazy, but I worried about Tall Guy who hadn't moved since lying down. If Whitetip were to put one foot on the bridge, it would collapse for sure.

The furry beast forced me to make up my mind. He leapt up and immediately scratched out at my police officer's left boot. His claw ripped through the leather like it was paper. Next, he grasped my rucksack in his jaw, shook me and flung me along the bridge towards Tall Guy. Multi-coloured toothbrushes scattered across the boards. 'Get off!' I shouted. 'I'm a black belt in karate.'

Dad, Kwasi and Short Guy shouted to distract the lion, and that worked for a brief moment, giving me time to scamper to Tall Guy. I reached him, dropped to the boards and shook him by his feet. 'Are you okay?' I asked, but there was no reply.

The lion roared at the men. Whitetip huffed and snorted at us. The lion turned his attention to the rhino and roared thunderously at Whitetip who snorted back at the giant cat. Whatever they had said to each other, the rhino must have upset the lion because he turned away from growling at the men and trotted towards us. His sharp fangs, revealed by his raised lip, were white as paper. Pity he still had *his* front teeth.

'Keep your head down,' I called to Tall Guy.

When the big cat reached me it jumped up and over both of us and landed on top of Whitetip. What a leap! And I thought he was just a worn out, old man-lion.

Whitetip turned and galloped off into the bushes, trying to shake the lion from its back and doing lots of snorting and huffing.

Kwasi helped me up and guided me to safety on the other side of the gorge. Meanwhile, Dad and Short Guy took an arm each and brought Tall Guy steadily to the other side of the ravine. The wood beneath their feet crackled and strained as they eased their way to safety.

'You're a brave girl, Deni, or completely mad,' Kwasi remarked as we reached the land, 'and possibly very lucky too.'

‘Lucky and brave aren’t the words I would use right now,’ said Dad. ‘But I possibly would agree with the “mad” bit.’ I felt he was disappointed in me. ‘Come here, Deni, you crazy thing,’ he said, and he gave me a loving hug. I could tell he was relieved that I had escaped without injury. He even photographed me holding my scratched boot. He held my sweaty hand tightly all the way to the village – and back. When we returned to the Land Rovers, there was no sign of either the old lion or Whitetip.

Back in England, the first thing we did was to send a *thank you* card to our African friends, with a picture of the bronze lions in London’s Trafalgar Square. I wrote, “These are the type of lions we like!”

Some days later we received a selfie from Kwasi with the message, “I now can eat an apple.”

A smile, the size of Fakenham, showed two new front teeth.

Solid gold.

15 Welcome Hero

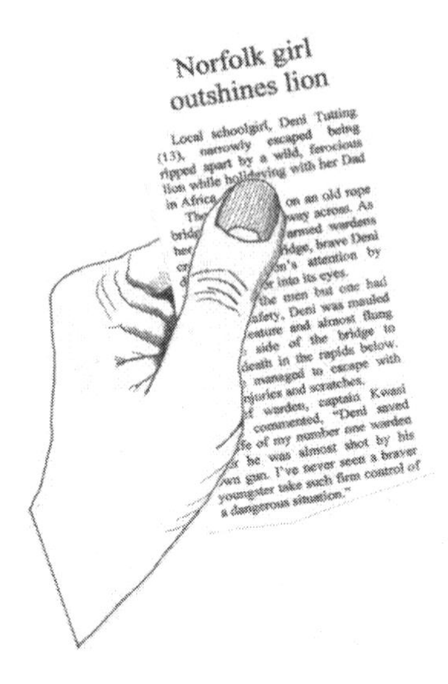

Norfolk girl
outshines lion

Local schoolgirl, Deni Tutting
(13), narrowly escaped being
ripped apart by a wild, ferocious
lion while holidaying with her Dad
in Africa … on an old rope
The … way across. As
bridg… armed wardens
he… ridge, brave Deni
… n's attention by
… e into its eyes.
… the men but one had
… afety. Deni was mauled
… eature and almost flung
… side of the bridge to
… death in the rapids below.
… managed to escape with
… njuries and scratches.
… warden, captain Kwasi
… commented, "Deni saved
… fe of my number one warden
… he was almost shot by his
… wn gun. I've never seen a braver
youngster take such firm control of
a dangerous situation."

I heard the giggle before I saw Gran. She stood in our front doorway, clapping as we pulled into the drive. 'The hero returns,' she said. Dad and I kissed and cuddled her. 'I've got something to show you, Deni – lion tamer!'

Gran had been busy at our house preparing a 'welcome home' tea. A meaty smell mixed with strawberry jam, greeted us as we dragged our suitcases inside. Shepherd's pie, my favourite; jam sponge, Dad's. She ushered us inside and made sure we settled on a seat with a drink. 'The food's almost ready. We're just waiting for Chloe and Lucy. They'll be over once they've cleaned up. Been to hockey.'

From Chloe next door, a loud 'Hi, Deni!' forced its way through our connecting wall. Gran picked up a newspaper from the coffee table. 'This is today's Daily Press. Just look at that headline – "Norfolk girl outshines lion." I guessed it could only be my Deni! Shall I read a bit of the report?'

Dad nodded. I clapped.

On went her reading glasses. She folded the paper and placed it on her lap. 'Now where did I put my glasses?'

'On your face,' said Dad.

She smiled, a bit embarrassed, I thought.

'"Local schoolgirl, Deni Tutting (13), narrowly escaped being ripped apart by a wild, ferocious lion while holidaying with her Dad in Africa. The lion, dozing on an old rope bridge, blocked the way across. As her dad and three armed wardens crossed over the bridge, brave Deni diverted the lion's attention by shining a mirror into its eyes.

'"Once all the men but one had passed to safety, Deni was mauled by the creature and almost flung over the side of the bridge to certain death in the rapids below. But she managed to escape with minor injuries and scratches.

'"Chief warden, captain Kwasi Larue, commented, "Deni saved the life of my number one warden after he was almost shot by his own gun. I've never seen a braver youngster take such firm control of a dangerous situation."'

'Isn't that a fantastic report?' said Dad.

'There's a photo too,' and Gran held it up so we could see it. 'You're holding a boot, Deni, and you seem a bit hot and bothered in the photo.'

'That's because a lion the size of a horse had just jumped over me. I'm in shock.'

'I emailed that photo to the Daily Press that same day, with some of the details. I thought it might help to convince Watchett your story is true,' said Dad.

'And it says here,' Gran continued, '"Over sixty thousand readers daily." Now that's a massive audience for you, sweetheart.'

She passed the newspaper to Dad. 'Tony, I'm a bit tired from all the cooking. Would you read out what her schoolmates said?'

'I'd love to,' and he scanned the report for the quotes. 'Here's one. "She's a very determined and capable girl, who's my bestest mate and really great at problem-solving and helping others. I'm not surprised she escaped from a lion." That's Chloe obviously. There's a quote from Danny Mulhouse. "She's wicked!"

'And, hang on, one more. "You've got to be careful with Deni Tutting – she often exaggerates things." Would you believe it? That's from Dirk Watchett.'

I sprang up like a pilot in an ejector seat that had just been ejected. My fists and teeth were clenched ready for battle. 'That interfering cow pat, Watchett. Why did they have to interview him? I'm gonna sort him out once and for all. First, he writes about me on posters, then he decorates our car with icing, then he bursts in on our radio session and now this!' I stamped a foot. 'He's the world's biggest lying toad. I shall stretch his neck from Cromer to Sheringham. And I do *not* exaggerate.'

'Take no notice of him and he'll go away,' Dad said.

'That's what many people say, but he's still here, spoiling things.' I knew Dad wasn't going to get involved. Mum would have gone straight to the headteacher and camped in her office until she sorted things out.

Gran spoke calmly. 'Sit back down, Deni. I thought it was a lovely report. Don't let that Dirk what's-his-name spoil it for you. Cut his bit out of the paper, but keep the rest in your souvenir box.'

Gran

We all sat back, in silence, with misery on our faces, when in burst the human tornado Chloe. She jumped into the middle of the room with arms outstretched and shouted, 'I'm in the newspaper!'

All three of us said together, 'We knowwwwww!' and the misery could be read on our faces.

'Did I say something wrong?' she asked.

It appeared that being a bit famous might have a good side, like news reports and telly, and a bad side, like schoolmates becoming jealous. I'd just have to make sure I got a bigger share of the good side.

Later, in my bedroom, I made a list:

FIVE THINGS I'M GOING TO DO WHEN I'M FAMOUS

a. Have a pet skunk trained to shoot smelly liquid at my enemies.
b. Put all my old clothes and school uniform through a shredder.
c. Dye my hair pink and green, striped.
d. Start a new search for the lost gold of Eldorado.
e. Fly to places where it is still yesterday and therefore live longer.

16 An Unwelcome Visitor

Within a few days, my home dramatically changed inside. It had been transformed. It was no longer an ordinary family home because Dad had turned it into *The Deni Tutting Picture Gallery*. Ever since my picture appeared in the newspaper, he had become obsessed with framing and displaying photo after photo which he named *Portraits of My Adventurous Daughter.*

Dad stood on a chair in the sitting room (Mum called it *the day room* and Dad called it *the lounge*). 'Could you hold this picture please, Deni, while I bang a nail in?'

Even Lucy came over a few times and hammered picture hooks in here and there. She and Dad smiled a lot when they were together. I think they are getting serious about each other because I saw Dad hold a door open for Lucy and he never did that for Mum (or for me).

'Okay, pass the picture, Deni.'

Fresh images of me stared down at me from every wall in every room. In the hallway, I held up that scratched boot. In the bathroom, I was soaking wet from hiding in the river Amazon. Here in the sitting room, I waved through the open window of a 4-wheel drive somewhere in Africa.

'Does that look straight to you?'

'Looks fine.'

'These pictures celebrate your survival skills,' he said, 'and your bravery.'

In the kitchen, I stood with Captain Blademan on the deck of Sea-ya. And halfway up the stairs, I threw snowballs in the Arctic.

Loads more photos, framed and unframed, rested against the sitting room wall waiting to go up. Sadly, those new images replaced all the old photos that had been taken away, stuffed into a box, and dumped behind the telly. I missed them already. Gone – a picture of me aged six receiving a present from Santa. Gone – Chloe and me at primary school with missing front teeth. Gone – arm-in-arm with Chloe at the top of the London Eye (my favourite photo). Gone – the old photo from the top landing. (I don't remember exactly who was in it, but Gran was.) Gran re-lived her memories through her photos. I supposed these new pictures would one day make my past more memorable. However, my eyes glared down at me from the frames and followed me around the room. I found my own face became annoying. What a relief it was when Dad sent me to the shop for more nails.

On returning to my house, I was about to shout, "I'm home," when I heard voices coming from the sitting room. Being nosey, I decided to listen in on the conversation. Very gently, I closed the front door. Leaving my jacket and shoes in the hallway, I crept to the sitting room door and listened. Two people talked.

'This photo is of Deni in Africa. Have you been to Africa?' (That sounded like Lucy's voice.)

'No.' (That sounded like a youngish male.)

'The furthest east we've been is Lowestoft,' said Lucy.

'Africa's south. Not east,' said the stranger. (He came across as rude.)

I recognised Lucy's voice, but not the visitor's. Why would Lucy show someone around the photo gallery? That's normally Dad's job. He loves boasting about me.

'Let's go to the kitchen. There's more in there,' she said.

I hid behind Dad's long raincoat hanging in the hallway, wrapping it tightly around me. My feet stuck out from beneath the coat, but I hoped they wouldn't be noticed. I listened out for the clomping of shoes as the couple crossed the hall to the kitchen.

I held my breath so that I could hear them talking. Lucy said, 'This photo was taken in Australia. Have you been to Australia?'

'No.'

'Me neither. But I've been to Lowestoft.'

'You mentioned that earlier,' the visitor said (I thought, in a dismissive way.)

'Let's go back to the hallway.'

I dashed from the protection of Dad's coat, on tiptoe, into the sitting room, intending to hide behind the couch. In my hurry, I knocked into the coffee table and some pens rolled off on to the floor. The visitor asked, 'What was that noise in the sitting room?'

'I didn't hear anything,' said Lucy. 'It might be our cat, Drainpipe. He often sneaks in here – any open window.'

'Has he been to Lowestoft?'

Lucy giggled.

Behind the couch, I made myself as small as I could, bringing my legs right in under my chin and tucking my arms tightly into my chest. I wished I could have squeezed *under* the couch.

The visitor stopped at the doorway and peered into the room. I couldn't see him, but I could hear him breathing. He'd better not come in and start looking for Drainpipe. I'd be so embarrassed to be found hiding like some sort of coward.

Lucy asked, 'Do you own a cat?'

'No.'

'You don't say a lot, do you?'

'I can hear your cat breathing,' said the visitor.

Lucy pushed past the visitor. 'If he's in here I'll find the little pest,' and she came in and ruffled the curtains. 'Drainpipe, are you there?' I saw the tip of her shoe when she came near the sofa. Fear of being discovered shrank me and I closed my eyes. My breathing came faster and my lungs became over-filled balloons.

'Why is he called Drainpipe?'

Lucy returned to the visitor standing in the doorway. 'When he was a kitten, he got stuck in the bend of our drainpipe and had to be cut free by the fire brigade. Chloe found him. Very upset she was.'

'When I was a kid we had a cat, black and white. It died. Got its tail caught in a bedroom door. Rolled all the way down the stairs and into a plant stand, causing the pot to fall on its head. Then it staggered into the road where it was grabbed and carried away by a bald eagle recently escaped from a zoo. The bird dropped our cat down a chimney.'

'Poor darling,' said Lucy. 'What was your cat's name?'

'Smokey.'

Lucy held back a smile.

'Your cat is not in here,' said the visitor. 'I'll go now, Mrs Clarke. Thanks for showing me the gallery.

That voice – I recognised it. I sucked in a lungful of air and a mouthful of carpet dust that tickled my throat. An almighty cough began forming in my chest. How *dare* he come into my *own* house – to spy on me.

'Goodbye Dirk. Thanks for visiting,' and she closed the front door, returned to the kitchen and fiddled with some plates. I coughed into my sleeve to deaden the sound, eased up from my hiding place and tiptoed to the hallway to grab my coat and shoes. I quietly opened the front door and, as though I'd just arrived, slammed it shut as noisily as I could and wailed, 'I'm home.'

Lucy peered out from the kitchen doorway, drying a plate with a tea towel. 'Hi Deni.'

‘Hi Lucy. Have you moved in?’

She giggled. ‘No. Your dad wanted me to show one of your schoolmates round the gallery. He just this minute left. You must have passed him on your way in. A nice lad, but a bit odd too!’

‘I didn’t see him. Who was he?’

‘He had a funny name. Dick, Duck, Dirk . . .’

‘. . . Watchett?’

‘That’s it. Do you know him?’

‘Yes, unfortunately. He’s the class snot nose.’

‘Is he not very nice?’

‘He can be a pest at times.’

‘I knew I’d heard the name before. Chloe’s talked about Watchett. Anyhow, as he was leaving, he made a strange comment. I haven’t a clue what he meant.’

‘What comment?’

‘He pointed to your scratched boot photo in the hall, hanging just behind you, and he said, “Deni *is* telling the truth after all.”’

17 Invasion of the Village Green

September, a new class, 9B. Chloe and I together as always. We vowed to work solidly for our new form teacher, Mrs Crow (nicknamed 'the lobster,' because she always wore red). She was very cool, popular with most pupils and a concerned listener. We liked the lobster. (Last term, she had a serious word with Gabby Trainer who called Chloe and me "street litter," after we crawled under her desk and tied her shoelaces together.)

The morning of that day is a blur, however, the afternoon turned out to be more memorable.

On returning to Little Sumpton after school, there was a surprise awaiting us. (You know I hate surprises.)

'What's all that on the Village Green?' I asked Chloe as we stepped down from the school bus. Normally, we'd be able to see our homes from the bus stop, but today we couldn't. Vans, lorries and cars were scattered and parked all over our end of the Green, totally blocking our view. What was going on?

There were two main rules for the Village Green that everyone reminded us of from an early age – no ball games and no cars. An ancient notice, in scrawly black ink on wood, listed what we *could* do on the Green;

By order of Her Gracious Majesty,
Queen Elizabeth the First,
this year of 1602

Any villager of Little Sumpton may be allowed forthwith to graze a herd of cows on the Green, up to the number of five beasts, whose horns have been blunted, provided the total of ye cows does not exceed twenty beasts in total. Strictly NO pigs.

Adults may …………… and children can ………….. if it is raining. (No one remembered what this rule said as it had been scrubbed off in places.)

Villagers may perform or partake in a maypole dance once a year on a Wednesday only. Girls in dresses that reach to the ground.

Villagers are permitted to set up stocks for the punishment of offenders.

Loud music should be played softly. (We think this rule is from modern times.)

'Is the fun fair arriving?' Chloe suggested. 'I can't see the bumper cars or the big wheel.'

‘I’m sure we would have been told if the fair was coming. We’d normally get a leaflet delivered.’

‘Perhaps it’s got something to do with your new photo gallery.’

‘Do you think so?’

Chloe pointed. ‘On the side of that long lorry it says BBC and it’s parked right in front of our house. D’you think the Queen’s coming here on her way to Sandringham?’

‘I wouldn’t expect the Queen to have any interest in visiting Little Sumpton.’

‘Someone could’ve died.’

‘Don’t say that, Chloe. It could come true.’ Suddenly, after that comment, I felt my leg strength weakening.

We crept slowly at the edge of the Green, trying to see what all the fuss was about without attracting attention. A crowd of roughly twenty people, some with film cameras on tripods, had gathered in front of our homes. When we got closer to home, a short-haired woman spotted us and shouted, ‘There she is,’ causing the whole group to turn and face us.

I looked at Chloe. ‘Do they mean *me*?’

The strangers ran towards us like a herd of deer. Some lifted their equipment and carried it as they ran, dodging between the vehicles. Within seconds, they had surrounded us and bombarded me with questions. Flashlights blinded me and I grew confused by everyone talking at once. I felt ready to topple over. I didn’t like them being so near. I could smell their musty raincoats and on their breath, stale beer, chips and cigarettes.

From all the talking and babbling, two or three questions managed to grab my attention; “Deni. Can you explain why your dad sent you across an old rickety bridge in Africa?” “Deni dearest, tell us about your injuries. Did the lion hurt you badly?" "How do you feel about your father putting your life in danger?"

I became a bit light-headed with all the talk and lights. I imagined myself trapped inside my old Birthday Box and the walls moved inwards and the air started to run out. Just as I almost ran out of breath, someone grabbed the top of my arm.

'All right, all right, you lot. Step back,' Dad said firmly, keeping an eye out for me and reaching me once again at a needy moment. He stood between me and Chloe and placed his arms around our shoulders.

'Now you news reporters and photographers should know Deni is just thirteen. You can't report about her without my permission and I don't like the questions about me putting my daughter in danger – it wasn't like that.'

I nodded in agreement.

Dad continued. 'I don't mind Deni answering a few questions – once I've heard them first. She needs time to think before she speaks. And you can take a few pictures – but not of Chloe. She wasn't there and I'm not her dad.'

There seemed a lot of interest in the story. A red-haired woman asked if I could appear on the *Early Morning Breakfast Show*. 'Can I Dad, please?' I would have loved to be on telly, but Dad said it would interfere with my schooling. He got a scowling stare from me for his comment.

I reckon I answered fifteen or so questions about my lion adventure. Dad was right, I did need thinking time. Even Chloe managed a question; 'Which gift did the villagers like most?'

I answered, 'The T-shirts, despite the lettering being upside down. They couldn't read the words and they didn't like the toothbrushes. They wanted electric ones!'

The questioning stopped abruptly and we went home. Chloe dashed into her house and Dad slammed our front door shut. 'Good riddance to that lot,' he said.

We collapsed onto the sofa. I had a feeling this publicity thing could be too demanding. People had begun talking about me. I heard them in the street, in shops, on the bus or wherever I went. I often crept nearer to them to listen. I needed to know what they thought of me. Were they impressed with my adventures? Did they believe my stories?

They'd say things like; "Isn't that the sawfish girl?" or "How could she fight off a lion – she's so tiny?" or "She should be locked up."

It was signing autographs I hated. Total strangers expected me to stop what I was doing and sign my name, often with a comment (To Wayne with fondest love. To Emily, who reads every day.) Or they'd just barge in and demand I sign.

At first, it was a laugh, signing for the younger kids at school. Then it became silly and everyone copied me and there were many fake ones going about. And lots of litter with my name on rolled around the playground on windy days. I got litter duty three times in one week!

Someone sold one of my autographs on eBay and made twenty quid. The headteacher got involved and autographing was banned after that.

As far as I could make out, there were three types of autograph collector. First, those with a proper autograph book who came prepared with their own pen. They were the serious collectors and for them I often added written comments. Then there were those fans with scrappy bits of paper (bus tickets, leaflets without a bit of writing space, sweet packets opened and reversed and impossible to write on). People in this group had no pen, borrowed mine and strolled off with it. Finally, the desperate, without paper, pen or intelligence, were autographed on hands, arms and legs, promising never to wash again.

Later, after eating a microwaved prawn pizza, my mobile received three texts. The first was Chloe's: "U were cool on Look East answering all those questions. Cya in morning 4 bus. CC (smiley face, kiss)." I replied, "U off 2 bed already? Get your H-work done Lazy. DT (two pizza slices, kiss)."

The second read: "My teddy's cuter than yours, and cuddlier." (From some anonymous loser.)

And a third read: "Looks like you really did fool that lion (smiley face with sunglasses)." ID withheld.

Nothing to worry about in those messages.

18 Run, Freeze or Fight?

Dad and I sat in the kitchen picking bits from his blackened pasta bake, sorting them into two piles: edible and burnt beyond recognition. ‘Deni, you need a break from all those reporters and photographers. We’re going to Australia again.’

‘Fabadoody!’

‘Only this time it’s on land, so no falling into the sea and dancing with sawfish, promise?’

‘How can I fall into the sea if I’m on land?’ I shovelled in a mouthful of pasta twists tasting of coal dust. ‘What film is it this time?’

‘*Dotty Picture Goes Missing.*’

We sang together, ‘Not it’s real title!’

'It's something to do with stealing a valuable aboriginal painting from the Sydney art museum. We'll be filming in a sacred area so we need permission from the tribal leader out there.'

'What's aborig-idal?'

'Abor-ig-i-nal. The people who were in Australia before campervans!'

'Ha, ha. What should I take to wear?'

'Your army kit.'

'Not that stuff again. It's all worn out with holes all over it. I'll look like one of those refugees from a war zone. You know how much I *hate* wearing it.'

'Well, it's very practical. We'll all be wearing combats. I'll buy a new set for you. What would you rather wear, a dress?'

'Cotton socks, please.'

'Okay, cotton socks.'

'Can Chloe come this time?'

'Not this time. Maybe on a future trip. We could organise a competition at school and the prize could be to come with us on our next trip. What do you think?'

'No thanks. Just take Chloe.'

The following Saturday, Chloe and I bussed into the city. We got off at the mall and took the glass lift to the third floor. I wanted some last minute items for the trip – clothes and Haribos. Dad gave me forty pounds to spend, ("Don't waste it."), so we headed straight for Shop-Till-U-Droop, attracted by their window display of pre-torn jeans against a background of flashing lights. However, we were distracted by someone shouting.

'I don't think they'll have your size.'

Dirk Watchett and two of his mates leant against the railings opposite the shops. They dropped tiny balls of rolled up paper on people as they passed below.

'Looking for a crocodile to fight, Deni?'

'Well if we find one we'll feed you to it,' Chloe quickly responded. I admired her wit and the speed she could fire it off.

'I'm not talking to you, Clarke. I'm talking to Superwoman, who's had all those escapes and shows it all off in her world famous picture gallery.' He sniggered and put his hands on his hips trying to look tough in front of his mates. He succeeded, but we knew he was jelly inside. He'd run laughing like a hyena if he had to face any of my wild animal dilemmas.

'You should put a video of you and your animals on YouTube, real evidence. Then we can get some real feedback.'

I was becoming annoyed now, on top of the bad feeling I still had following Watchett's invasion of my house. 'Just go away. I don't want your advice. Do you think I'd have time to film myself fighting for my life? The only video I'll be uploading will be of you being kicked down the escalator.'

'Unless you intend to shop here for a new dress, you'd better clear off,' Chloe quipped. His bodyguards laughed.

We'd had enough of Watchett so Chloe and I dashed into the clothes shop where we guessed he wouldn't follow. Glaring at us through the window, he pulled faces as if he came from a page of emojis. He left a large blob of red bubble gum stuck on the glass in the shape of a smile.

Australia was a long way from Little Sumpton. Our three campervans turned off the main highway and bounced along a powdery dirt track. My van, the size of a bus, had six beds, toilet, shower and a kitchen with a fridge packed with bottles of fizzy water.

Dad said the plan was to visit old tribal lands, which had some spectacular natural scenery.

I never realised until now that when it's winter in England, it's summer out here in Australia! It's also the bottom of the world and we're upside down and yet we hadn't dropped off the planet. Gravity worked just the same here as it did back home. I noticed, however, the local accent was different, but thankfully everyone spoke English. There were some words we didn't use in England and I couldn't say the names of some of the places, such as Talinguru Nyakunytjaku.

When we stopped for the first night in the middle of nowhere, Timmy, our guide, began to prepare supper as he was also our cook. He taught me some Australian words as we relaxed around his smoking campfire. 'Food is kept in my *tucker-bag,* Deni, and food is *tucker*,' he said, removing some tins and packets. 'Open fire cooking in the traditional style uses a pot called a *billycan*. You see it has a handle so we can hold it over the fire.'

'What are we having?'

'Dried snake and possum burgers.'

'Yuk. I'm not eating that!' Everyone around the fire laughed.

'Only joking,' said Timmy. 'It's kangaroo meat and roots. All local produce. Makes a fantastic stew.'

'Kangaroo? You can't eat kangaroo!'

'We do sometimes. You'll *love* it. Tastes like chicken. Makes you jump all night.' (More laughter.)

Not wanting to join in with that meal, I sneaked off in disgust. I had my own favourite food anyway; a giant chocolate bar, which I kept to myself and ravenously tucked into whenever I liked. I had to keep it wrapped in clothes as it tended to melt in the heat.

Later, as dusk set in, Dad tossed out a large bulky canvas bag from inside our van. It landed at my feet with a clump. 'That's for you, Deni.'

'What is it?' Hoping it wasn't what I thought it was.

'Your sleeping bag and tent.'

'What do you mean, tent?' I grumped, folding my arms. 'I'm sleeping in the van.'

Dad popped his head out of the van door. 'You're sleeping in a tent because you're the only girl.'

'Oh great! And I bet I have to put it up too.'

'Easy for a thirteen-year-old *outbacker*.'

It was no use arguing. I grabbed the bag, just able to lift it, and stormed off. I wasn't happy at having to put up a tent at this time of day, in this heat. I was even more concerned after what Timmy told me.

'Don't go too far into the *bush*, Deni. There are *dingoes* around these parts. They like fresh meat.'

'Fresh meat! Do you mean *me*? And what are dingoes anyway?'

'Wild dogs,' Timmy said. 'They can be unfriendly but remember, animals cannot be cruel. They can be hungry and attack you for food and that makes them seem cruel. They've been known to attack humans.'

Timmy knew all there was to know about the Australian *outback*. His face showed a lifetime of experience and wisdom in its cracks and crinkles. I stood and stared at him as he picked up a half-burnt stick from near the fire and sketched a dingo in the dirt. 'Watch out for the jaws. Like metal vices they are, really strong. We say, "Don't look a dingo in the eye or he'll have you in a pie!"' And he stabbed the stick into the dingo's neck.

'Typical,' I moaned. 'I have to sleep in a poxy tent and fight off savage wild dogs all night! Great. Just what I needed – *not*.'

Some trip this turned out to be.

‘Oh, and Deni,’ Timmy added as I was leaving, ‘hang any food you’ve got high up so the dingoes can’t reach it.’

I found a clear spot of land where I put up the tent, unrolled the sleeping bag and sorted out my clothes, pyjamas, toothbrush, alarm clock and water bottle. Into a carrier bag I put three bags of prawn crisps, a family packet of ginger biscuits, one tin of Devon custard, a double chocolate Swiss roll, four wagon wheels, half a jar of chocolate spread, two Double Deckers and a giant packet of Haribos. I tied the bag of goodies to a branch about two metres off the ground, as Timmy had advised. Next to my bed I placed my special half bar of chocolate for emergencies, and then I went behind a tree to brush my teeth.

Later, Dad came by to say goodnight. ‘See you at seven, Deni,’ he called out, but I put on a false snore and pretended to be asleep. I was still cross with him. I almost regretted giving back his wedding ring.

I slept without waking until it started to get light. I had been dreaming of Timmy cooking a small crocodile over a campfire and Dad poking it with a tent pole when I was woken by someone or something fiddling with my tent door zip. I sat up in my sleeping bag and heard heavy breathing followed by scratching at the zip. I looked around for a weapon but found only a toothbrush.

Pointing the toothbrush at the door, I asked, ‘Who’s there? Go away, I’ve got a toothbrush, er, gun.’

My threat had no effect. Whoever it was continued to scratch and scrape at the zip. In a shadow cast upon the door, I saw a rabbit’s head, a pear-shaped body and big ears. Too tall to be a dog and definitely not human. It could only be – a kangaroo.

Perhaps it was after my half bar of chocolate. I reached over for the bar and threw it at the tent door shouting, 'Take it if you want it,' but then realised that kangaroos probably don't understand English.

My actions and words only seemed to encourage the animal further. Somehow it managed to unzip my door completely and stuck its rabbit-like head inside my tent. There was no other exit. I couldn't even sneak under the tent walls because of the built-in groundsheet. I was sealed inside my canvas tent of doom.

Pulling my sleeping bag up to my chin, I hoped it would protect me. Then, in the early dawn light, I saw the monster clearly. It had small front legs and giant back ones – a bit like a T-rex. I'd seen kangaroos hopping about on our journey up here, but had never managed to get this close to one.

The intruder hopped towards me. Its head scraped the tent ceiling. I felt the ground shake and the tent shudder as the beast moved. Hissing and sticking out its tongue, it jumped on to my sleeping bag. I felt its tremendous weight crushing down on me.

I had three choices – run, freeze or fight. My brain said roll up and pretend to be dead. I chose to fight and head-butted the visitor in the chest. It turned and whacked me with its huge secret weapon – a muscular tail as thick as a human leg. I was sent flying out of my sleeping bag and across the tent. I went for it again and tried to wrestle it to the ground and make my escape. But rabbit face was too quick and powerful. I couldn't get past it to the door.

We grappled on the floor and I noticed the chocolate bar I'd thrown earlier. The beast must have come in for that, so I grabbed it and stuffed it into the roo's face shouting, 'Eat that you bloated bunny!' But it didn't give up its attack. My muscles soon weakened against the kangaroo's strength as it pinned me to the ground.

Thrashing about wildly for anything I could use as a weapon, my hand landed on my little alarm clock. I grabbed the clock and saw it was one minute to seven. That was almost up time. I pulled open the beast's pouch on its belly and stuffed the alarm clock deep down inside it. Both of us stopped fighting and stared at each other. I can only imagine that the beast was shocked at me touching it inside its very private pouch (for baby kangaroos only).

Almost immediately, from deep inside the pouch, there came a piercing buzz as my seven o'clock alarm went off on full volume. The kangaroo went berserk, slapping its pouch and crying. I shouted, 'Get lost!' and succeeded in shooing it out of the tent. I listened for the electronic buzz which grew fainter and fainter as the panicked beast hopped further away. I heard it crash into a couple of trees and trip over a few bushes. Next time, matey, pick on someone your own size.

Two minutes that alarm went off for! Two minutes of misery for the nasty monster who wanted my chocolate. It can look forward to that alarm every morning, *and* it had a ten-year battery!

On returning to the city, Australian TV interviewed Dad and me about the kangaroo attack. We ended up on the main news where my ordeal was treated as a bit of a joke ("An English tourist got into a fight with . . ."). I suppose it appeared comical, but I don't remember laughing at the time.

Dad, Timmy and I came under a bit of pressure from the presenter of *Breakfast on the Beach,* a popular TV morning show. We were in the street outside our hotel when she turned up with a cameraman and asked, 'Why leave a thirteen-year-old girl, in a tent, in the outback, on her own? Isn't that asking for trouble?'

Dad tried to answer, 'Well, er . . . as she was the only female . . .'

'Were you being irresponsible?'

Timmy spoke, 'Not far from Deni's tent I remained awake keeping watch. When the kangaroo got into the tent, I stayed out so as not to frighten the creature. Kangaroos are nervous animals. I might have spooked it. Anyway, within a minute or so Deni had the problem fully under control. No worries.'

The interviewer seemed happy with Timmy's answer. Later on, I caught up with Timmy. 'Thanks for looking out for me,' and I showed him my half medal. 'Do you have the other half of this?'

'Deni, I hate to disappoint you, but I am not your hero with the matching half. I have something like it though.' He delved into his kitbag and pulled out a claw, fixed to a golden keyring. 'The crocodile that owned this claw attacked me while I slept. This is my souvenir of the fight I had that night. I believe it brings me good luck.'

'We both carry lucky charms!'

'You're amazing, Deni. The whole country is talking about you! What's more, you defeated that kangaroo single handed. If you continue this way you'll end up with your own TV show!'

'Yeah,' I replied, 'Deni's Term-Time Trips.'

'Or how about, Deni's Daring Duels?'

I liked all the attention. The hotel staff made an extra effort for me by opening doors and calling me "hero," and the receptionist told me I was "a top-notch kidda!"

Life was becoming rather busy, but how much fuss could I take? On the negative side, photographers and reporters followed me almost all day long and that was annoying. Questions, questions, questions. "What's your favourite food? Which pop stars do you like? What do you enjoy most about Australia?"

I wanted to go home but Dad insisted we have a rest. He had booked an apartment in the Hotel Europa and planned to visit the Great Barrier Reef and the Sydney Opera House. He promised me a barbecue on the beach with real food – not snake, possum or kangaroo!

And Dad had another reason for staying on . . .

19 Greetings from Afar

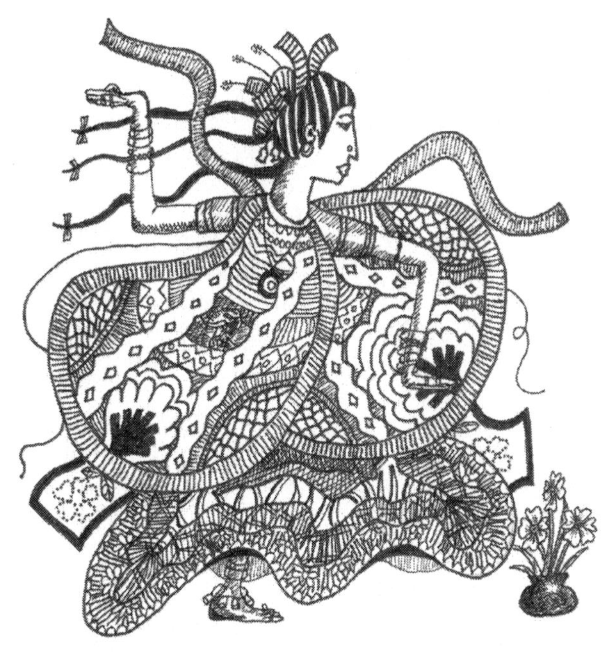

The Hotel Europa's phone, on the wall near Dad's double bed, buzzed and startled me. 'Send her up please,' Dad said down the phone. 'That's okay, we've got loads of space . . . yes, of course we'll put it all back.' He plonked the phone down and dashed about the room tidying up a shoe here, a towel there. 'We've got a visitor on the way up.'

'I gathered that much. Not another reporter, is it?'

'I don't think so, unless she's changed jobs since I last saw her.'

A woman visitor – could it be Mum? I tidied my hair in the bathroom.

A rapid knocking on the door stopped Dad from clearing up. He opened the door and in marched a man who had to stoop to get through the doorway. He was dressed in a wildly colourful costume, mostly of orange and yellow. He stood to one side of the door, bowed to us and clapped three times.

Bells around their ankles tinkled when two boys entered wearing delicate and colourful costumes that could have been made from butterflies' wings. Tall Man clapped again, and the boys lifted and shifted tables, chairs and lamps. Anything not attached to the floor the boys hauled back to the wall. They worked fast like those busy ants that carry leaves in the jungle. Dad and I jumped onto the big bed to keep away from all their movement. When they'd finished, a clear space had been created in the centre of the room. The boys took up positions either side of the doorway, as straight as soldiers on guard.

'Is this part of the film you're working on?' I asked Dad.

'No. It's all new to me.'

Tall Man clapped again, four times. In she came, a perfumed breeze, a smooth-skinned girl in a costume of sunlight. Wrist bangles spun and dangles jangled as she danced and glided above the floor. Diamonds in her gold rings, mother-of-pearl buttons and hundreds of sequins in her costume sparkled and dazzled my eyes. Her glossy black hair swayed under a scarf of silk. She moved like a whirlwind, like a ballerina, twisting on her pointed toes, and she scattered sweet-scented rose petals from a KFC party bucket.

Dad smiled. Tall Man clapped once and four men in white suits entered, each carrying a musical instrument. They settled into a corner, set down a carpet, sat cross-legged upon it and played a melodic tune, which I had not heard before. With an enchanting rhythm and piercing notes, the sounds formed a musical painting of a far-away homeland and missed loved ones.

'They're playing *We are the Champions,*' Dad whispered.

Tall Man called out, 'Please be upstanding for her royal highness . . . Queen Kaarma the 17th of the kingdom of Kaarmastan.'

We bounced off the bed and stood as asked. A skinny old lady waddled in as though she was lost. (I remembered Queen Kaarma from Dad's story on the yacht, but this pensioner couldn't be the Queen – she looked too old and frail.) She wore flashing-light jelly shoes, beige shorts and a T-shirt saying "PARTY TIME – YOU LUCKY DUDES." If she had a bucket and spade she'd be ready for the beach. I stepped in front of her to stop her coming any further into the room.

'Excuse me, but can you leave? We're expecting a queen.'

I grabbed the visitor's arm and was about to throw her back out into the corridor when Tall Man picked me up by my ankles and dangled me upside-down in front of the scraggy old tourist who, from my viewpoint, resembled a hairy boiled egg. 'Please, do not manhandle her royal highness,' Tall Man said.

'Don't worry, Harish. I know about Deni. She reacts quickly to dangers. That is to be expected. Now put her down carefully.'

'I'm so stupid,' I mumbled from a heap on the floor.

'Do not dwell on unpleasantries, Deni,' said the Queen, and she tottered over to Dad, who had been enjoying my silly mistake in grabbing hold of the Queen, judging by the huge smile that took up most of his face.

'Tony, we meet again. This time in more comfortable surroundings.' They shook hands and hugged.

'It's been too long, Your Majesty. I'm glad you are able to come and see us.'

'I have my own jet. I can go anywhere I like.'

‘May I introduce my daughter, Deni?’ and he nudged me towards the Queen. I was still embarrassed about having rugby tackled her.

I felt that the old friends had a lot to talk about so I chilled with the band. They let me play each instrument. My favourite, the four-stringed tanpura, looked a bit like a stretched guitar. I fell in love with its sound. (Later, Queen Kaarma promised to send me a brand new one in the post.)

I watched Dad give the Queen a black box, like a wristwatch box but longer. I asked him later what was inside the box. ‘A little gift, that’s all.’ Which meant it was a secret, so I didn’t continue trying to find out. I had a good idea what the box contained.

On the plane back to England, just as the steward announced that we should turn off our electronic devices and mobile phones, I got a mysterious text – number withheld. “Saw you on the late TV news. A cool story! (with a smiley face and a pair of clapping hands).”

It must have been from Chloe.

20 Bye Plane

'The Gallery is no more!' I shouted, as soon as I woke up. Three months of *me* glaring down at *me* staring up at *me* had driven *me* mad. My fourteenth birthday wish was to have the new photos removed and the old ones returned. Anyway, guests were due (Gran, Lucy and Chloe) and I felt sure they'd had enough of bees, lions and kangaroos too.

Opening twelve birthday cards could have been the start of a splendid day, but the cards failed to cheer me up because Mum hadn't sent one. To be honest, most of the cards were boring (*To my darling daughter . . . To my favourite girl . . .*) with those ridiculous rhymes. Chloe's card caused a smile – an old, scraggy sheep in a muddy field with the caption *Have a long and happy retirement.*

The cards put me in a rotten mood that continued to grow throughout the morning. Like the hideous red spot that appeared overnight on my chin; a bubbling ruby volcano about to erupt and I bet it would last at least a week. Some birthday gift.

Gran arrived early at nine o'clock to bake a jam sponge. 'Get the oven on,' she called from the front door. I heard the clashing of her baking trays, jars and large silver cutlery. Her voice must have alerted Chloe next door who arrived shortly after.

'Happy birthday, Den. See if you can find a use for this,' she said, thrusting my present at me, almost throwing it like it might go bang.

I turned it in my hands. 'Feels like a book.'

She'd purposefully wrapped it badly in cheap *Happy 60th Anniversary* paper from Little Sumpton stores (20p a roll). Its wonky sellotape felt sticky on the outside. I tugged and tore the wrapping. 'I was right. It *is* a book! *"Learn to speak Flemish in more than twelve months."*' I smiled. 'That can go straight in the bin . . . only kidding . . . souvenir box.'

'I knew you'd like it,' she said, sarcastically.

For Chloe's next birthday (and don't you tell her), I'd bought her a green teapot with *Granny's Cuppa* in large pink letters on both sides. And to cover the pot – a hand-knitted, orange tea cosy I picked up in a charity shop for thirty pence.

Next to arrive was Lucy. A delicious tang of lemony sweetness filled the air as she entered the hallway carrying a tray of yum yums. 'Morning, girls. Happy Deniday.' It took her three round trips to deliver all the scrummy cakes to the sitting room table. They just begged to be eaten; Viennese slices, chocolate eclairs,

Bakewell tarts and mini jam doughnuts, all homemade in my honour, sat waiting to be scoffed. Lucy's baking skills deserved an award.

'By the way, girls. To put a stop to your questions and gossip – Tony and I are "going out," but we're not engaged or anything – just enjoying each other's company as we're both single. Ok?'

Chloe and I, with raised eyebrows, mouthed "oooh twins."

It appeared that some surprises could be very acceptable.

Before anyone arrived this morning, Dad had destroyed a pack of eight pancakes in an attempt to make breakfast. He microwaved them almost to extinction. I joined him and sat at the table. 'I think we should rename breakfast "break-away." You break it; I throw it away.'

'Hey, sour face,' he said. 'I'm thinking about a birthday trip for you.'

'I'm not in the mood for any trips. I'll get into real trouble if you keep taking me out of school in term-time. It's against the government's new rules. We could be fined loads of money.' He struggled to remove burnt food from a grill pan with a pair of pliers.

'It's all under control, Deni. I've okayed it with your headteacher. She sees our trips as a useful learning experience. And she's proud of your bravery. She told me that your skill in dealing with dangerous animals has given the school a boost in the ratings.'

'Well, this is an important year for me Dad. I've got course work and exams. I can't take loads of time off.'

'You worry too much. I'll make sure not to arrange any trips during exam time.' He shifted in his chair.

‘Well, *you* don’t have to do the studying, do you?’ I plunged a teaspoon deep into a jar of strawberry jam and plonked a dollop onto my rock hard pancake. The spoon slipped from my hand and crashed into the plate, splitting it in half. Tiny sharp pieces flew across the table.

‘My little girl. You’re fourteen today. Happy birthday,’ he said chirpily, but his singing and dancing attitude failed to brighten me up. ‘I’ve arranged a very special surprise trip for you later in the week,’ he said, adding a sideways glance and a smile.

‘You know I hate *most* surprises. What is it?’

‘Secret.’

‘Give me a clue, go on,’ I begged.

‘Well, it’s something to do with the sky.’

I played around with the jam lumps on a large fragment of my broken plate. It seemed he’d brought back the dreaded Birthday Box game – all the guessing but without the box. Most surprises were just cruel jokes in disguise.

‘Bungee jumping,’ I suggested.

‘Not likely.’

‘Painting landscapes with loads of clouds?’

‘Too messy.’

‘Give me another clue,’ I begged.

‘No. You’ll guess it, then it won’t be a surprise.’

He wouldn’t tell me anything else about my birthday trip.

When the special surprise day came, Dad drove us south towards London. Along the way, I searched for signs that would give me a clue as to what he had planned. *Dinosaur Park, Forest Cycle Track, Paintballing, Duxford Air Museum* – we sped past them all.

'Are we nearly there yet?' I asked with a yawn, feeling guilty that boredom had set in.

'About forty-five minutes and you'll see. It will all be worth the wait.'

'You're tired of driving. Want me to take over?' He laughed at that.

We stopped at a services for a cheese sandwich. Two bites and I'd had enough so I kept the rest for later. I supposed I should have been grateful that Dad was giving me his time and attention. After all, wasn't that what I'd always wanted? And when he was really needed he'd always appear, doing his fatherly duties without complaining.

We finally arrived at Elstree Aerodrome, somewhere north of London. Dad told me "aerodrome" was an old-fashioned word for airfield.

As we entered the airfield half a dozen small planes and a few helicopters came into view. 'It's a helicopter ride!' I exclaimed, trying to sound enthusiastic.

'Not that. Something more . . . historical.'

'A hot air balloon? Microlight? Hang-glider? Am I getting close?' Anything going up in the air would be fantastic. 'Oh, Dad, tell me! Put me out of my misery.'

We parked next to a huge building with a curved roof where aircraft were stored. Outside this building stood an old, yellow, two-winged plane, which I reckoned was from the First World War. Surely a go in that thing wasn't to be my birthday present!

We got out of the car to be greeted by an old guy with oil-stained hands. He'd been fiddling with bits of engine. I couldn't tell which was older, plane or man. Both could have come straight out of a black and white silent movie.

'Captain Lord Abbeville?' Dad asked as they shook hands.

'Good wind for a super flight,' he beamed. 'Welcome to Incredible Flying Wrecks.' My jaw dropped.

We approached the plane. I felt sick. It looked as though it had been through *both* world wars and appeared to have been made out of wood and cloth! I raised my eyebrows and pointed. 'You won't catch me in that lemon.'

'It's not a lemon, young lady. It's a rare 1932 twin-seater Tiger Moth biplane. And you're very privileged to fly in her today. She's been fully restored to her former glory,' boasted Lord Abbeville, adding, 'Never crashed.'

'I should hope not,' I moaned, and glanced scornfully at Dad. 'But does it fly?'

'Of course it flies, like a soaring majestic eagle whose wings . . .'

'. . . are held together with thin sticks. Do we need two wings?'

'Most old planes were given two or even three wings. That's how it was in the early days. Now stop fretting, miss.'

My comments had upset the ancient airman. I'd better calm it down a bit. I quietly asked Dad, 'Are you really expecting me to go up in that kite? It's made out of old bed sheets.'

'You'll love it once you're up in the clouds. It does loop-the-loops, flies upside-down and dive-bombs.' Dad had obviously done his homework.

'I'll only go if it's quick – and with a parachute.'

'No parachute, missy – against regulations,' said the captain.

'That floppy moth should be against regulations more like,' I said, pouting.

Lord Abbeville checked his watch. 'Now let's not have any sulking. Here,' he said, handing me a bundle of old flight gear that should have been in a museum, 'put these on.'

I had to wear an extra-large fleecy white jacket with *Flying Ace* printed on the back in worn gold letters, a leather flying cap and a pair of split lens goggles (which I could keep as a souvenir). Dad laughed when he saw what I had to wear.

'Right, missy, hop in – you're in front.'

I had no wish to be a pilot. 'Am I driving?'

'I'll do all the driving from the seat behind. All *you* need to do is sit back and enjoy the view over the city. You can look down on the London Eye.'

I climbed up and squeezed into the red leather front seat. Comfortable it should have been but I had a sharp spring to sit on.

Dad filmed us and waved as we putt-putted down the runway. I shouted to his lordship, 'Shall I get out and push?'

I closed my eyes as we lifted magically into the air. Worryingly, both wings wobbled up and down as we left the land behind and just made it over a wall of trees.

From a fantastic viewpoint at the front, houses and cars shrank to the size of toys as we chugged higher and higher. Fields were rectangles of yellow, brown and green, while rivers and roads became snakes. I started enjoying the experience. (Thanks Dad, for a wonderful gift. Sorry I ever objected.)

I turned around and shouted, 'It's brilliant, captain,' but I felt sure the noise of the engine drowned me out.

However, he announced that we were to do a loop-the-loop, which I knew meant a bit of upside-down stuff.

The old Tiger Moth strained as she climbed in to the loop. Blue smoke trailed behind us. My aching tummy had a fight with itself because everything suddenly appeared in the wrong place. The ground was up, the sky was down and I was inside-out. Were we flying backwards? I was scared, especially when we stopped in mid-air at the peak of the loop.

I tumbled out of my seat, screaming!

His Lordship stretched out a hand for me, but all I managed was to give him a quick high-five.

Falling and diving through the air, I woke up in a dream of horror. I *was* falling but I refused to believe it. The banana plane putt-putted away into the distance without me. I should have been in that plane but I wasn't. Instead, I was really falling, and fast. Gravity became my enemy.

'Thanks a lot, captain,' I struggled to shout but failed, unable to catch my breath in near-freezing conditions.

Then I remembered a TV programme about skydiving. To slow down, you had to stretch out your arms and legs. I did that, like a starfish, and I found more control and levelled my body.

Below me a peaceful world went about its normal business, unaware of my life-threatening situation. And as for that talisman! No one could possibly save me up here.

I remembered a news item. Didn't a passenger plane land safely on the surface of a river last year? And all the passengers were unhurt. I reckoned that lakes and clumps of trees could make a soft landing for me. Perhaps I should aim for one of those. I had about thirty seconds before smashing in to the ground.

Something distracted me – a movement, a rustle, in the corner of my right eye. Black and white, almost silent and flapping. It circled around, nearly touching me with its wing tip. A giant bird with a four-metre wingspan – an albatross. I had to get closer. (25 seconds till impact.)

From inside my jeans pocket, I pulled out my unfinished cheese sandwich. With a firm grip on it, I held it out towards the encircling albatross, waving it about hoping to attract the bird. (20 seconds till impact.)

It peaked at the sandwich then looked away, but quickly looked back. It turned sharply above me and gulped half of the sandwich.

At that moment I grasped hold of both of its feet. It squawked. I dangled under the bird like it was a living hang-glider. (15 seconds till impact.)

I could smell soil and grass. The albatross flapped its enormous wings and adjusted to its new heavy load. It just managed to keep us both up until I landed gently, running on a freshly ploughed field. I set the bird free.

'I love you, albatross! You saved my life!' I called after it. My legs had no strength left in them. I collapsed on to a hard clump of brown soil. I sat there for a while admiring the patterns left by the plough and tractor. I picked up a handful of dirt, kissed it and put it into my jacket pocket. What were chances of meeting an albatross?

The peace I had in being alone was shattered when the Tiger Moth roared over my head and twisted into a victory roll. Lord Abbeville waved to me and smiled.

'Walter! Walter!' someone shouted. A black labrador crept up behind me and licked my ear. The voice asked, 'How did you come to be in the middle of my field?'

'I dropped in by albatross.'

'Oh yeh! And I suppose you're waitin' for a fully dressed Indian elephant to take you home, eh?'

As we walked to the farmer's truck, he listened to the albatross story. On the bumpy ride back to the aerodrome, I told my kangaroo story. I don't think he believed either story, but Walter did. He wagged his tail at all the exciting bits.

Dad was delighted to see me. He gave me such a massive hug. ‘It’s all on film – the entire event from take-off to you grabbing the albatross’s feet. Unfortunately, your landing was hidden by trees. I’ve already put it on YouTube.’

And as I got ready for bed, Dad said, ‘I’ve just looked on YouTube and our video has had over a hundred-thousand hits! Deni Tutting – you are becoming famous!’

“Famous” sounded like a lot of hassle.

21 Stories and Lies

The old yellow school bus rumbled along the icy Norfolk lanes. We returned to grim reality after the Christmas break. The albatross incident seemed like it had happened to another person, not me.

Chloe and I sat at the back of the bus where it was warmer. I asked, 'Have you made a New Year's resolution?'

'I'm giving up chocolate.'

'No way! Are you joking?' Chloe and chocolate were like Booty and fur; never apart.

'Well, no chocolate yesterday is the best I've managed so far. What's your resolution?'

'Mine's more of a quest than a resolution. I want to find out who my talisman partner is. It's not you by any chance, is it?' Chloe tightened the scarf around her neck. I took hold of her scarf with thumb and forefinger and lifted it slightly to see if she had a chain on.

'It isn't me. I'm never there when you need saving. It's more likely to be your dad – he's always nearby when you're in danger.'

'You're probably correct, but show me your neck anyway.'

She pursed her lips and moved a little away from me. 'I only want to see if you're wearing the matching half medal.'

'Trust, Deni. You'll just have to believe me.' She turned away and gazed out the window.

I changed the subject and mentioned the text I got yesterday.

'Why would your mum contact you now? You haven't seen her since you were twelve. That's two years ago.'

'I'm not sure I want to have texts from her after so long. She's had plenty of time to call me over the years but she never did. I suppose she's got her reasons for not contacting me. I'm getting on so well with Dad at the moment that I don't want to upset things by getting in touch with Mum. He wouldn't like that.'

'You've got a new phone and number. How could she get hold of your new number?'

'I don't know. Maybe it wasn't Mum after all. Anyway, I'm changing my number again. Everyone knows it. All sorts of people phone me or text me asking for details about my trips. All this publicity stuff is getting me down. I'm fed up with my little bit of fame, Chloe. I want my own peaceful life back, as it used to be.'

'You chose this lifestyle! You've got the whole world following your every move – something you've always wanted – radio, newspapers, TV, internet. It's all Deni Tutting, Deni Tutting, Deni Tutting. Now you say you don't want it anymore! Make your mind up, sweetie.'

At the last stop before school, the bus picked up half a dozen kids, including Danny Mulhouse, who scrambled aboard with his massive, wide smile. 'Ay-up, Georgie boy,' he said to the driver. Strange. The driver's name was Mike. It said "Mike" on the ID card dangling around his neck.

Danny headed straight for me at the back of the bus and whispered, 'I need to tell you somethink in-portant, Deni. Catch yous two later.'

Just as we stepped off the bus at the school gates, a bunch of reporters and photographers swooped on us, probably looking for a new angle on the albatross story. I covered my face with my school bag. A reporter, fully armed with a microphone, recorder and camera, nudged me and asked, 'What's this about you going to the South Pole on your next trip, Deni?'

'I've no idea about any trip. Can you please leave me alone?'

Others called out, 'Deni, Deni, look this way,' and flashed their cameras but got no smiles from me today. Chloe took more interest in being photographed than I did.

A herd of younger pupils screamed and waved from behind the playground railings while the duty teacher, Mr Ford (nickname 'Fiesta'), clapped when he recognised me. The kids and staff were welcoming, whereas the press people were plainly annoying with their repetitive questioning.

Chloe smiled (falsely) and tried to get into the photo shots. Her attitude annoyed me a bit. She spoke too willingly, too eagerly. 'My name's Chloe Clarke and I think you should leave Miss Tutting alone. In addition, I am available for interview at any time,' she said in her usual, over-the-top and over-confident manner.

'Don't encourage them, Chloe. They'll pester you and then reject you once they grow tired of you.' I grabbed her sleeve and pulled her away.

We raced up the steps and into school to seek the safety of the building. Halfway along the main corridor, Dirk Watchett emerged from one of the empty classrooms, all smiles as usual and up to no good I assumed. He tauntingly called out, 'The famous celebrity's in the building. Autographs will be given for a small fee.'

He blocked our way by standing in front of us with arms outstretched. 'Not now, Watchett. I'm not in the mood for your crazy games,' I said, and brushed past swinging my bag at him and missing his spotty chin by millimetres.

'Good shot,' he barked. 'Planning more half-truths to scare the little ones?'

'Hands off my mate, Watchett, or I'll smack ya. You half-baked, half-pint, half-wit,' added Chloe, shaking a fist in his face.

'Can't a poor lad have a brief moment for a pleasant conversation?'

'Since when has anything you've ever said been pleasant?' Chloe responded. She always could throw a whacking verbal punch.

He watched us reach the swing doors at the Year 9 end of the corridor before calling, 'Did you get my texts?'

Chloe and I stopped, released the doors and turned to face the creep. 'What texts?'

Watchett grinned, turning the corkscrew deeper into my brain. 'The one on the plane and the *"luckiest girl"* text.'

I was livid. After all the worry those nameless texts had caused me, it was Watchett who sent them. My eyes became daggers aimed straight at his head. I screamed, 'Don't ever text me again Watchett, or I'll report you for cyberbullying.'

'I've not bullied you. I've been nice.' He sounded pathetic.

'I call it bullying, so it *is* bullying. Don't come over all innocent. You're just playing with my feelings and I don't need that right now – or at any time.'

'Well, sor-ry.'

Chloe pointed at Watchett, stabbing the air with her sharp, ruby painted fingernail, 'Quit it, Watchett. Can't you see she's upset?'

She put her arm over my shoulder and we made a quick exit through the swing doors. I cried, but not in front of Watchett. Never.

Chloe had been mistaken for me recently, which was not surprising given our similarities in looks. She was often with me when photographers and reporters poked their hairy noses in. How were they to tell us apart? We probably were as attention-seeking as each other and I hoped Chloe didn't feel motivated by jealousy. I *know* she spoke to some Daily Press reporters and pretended to be me! She craftily told them a false story – how I escaped from a herd of long-horned highland cows by singing *Old MacDonald had a Farm.* That was not my style. Such stories make me out to be some sort of wimp.

How did her lying come to my attention? There was a witness: Danny Mulhouse. He got things wrong occasionally but I trusted him on this matter. He'd been standing next to Chloe when she told her false story and he gave me a copy of the Daily Press report.

I read the cow report to Chloe one lunchtime while we chomped into a box full of Lucy's home-crafted fairy cakes. 'The headline said, *"Old MacTutting tricks herd with a song."*' The more I read the greater her fidgeting became and the faster she ate.

When I'd finished reading, I said, 'That's one escape story that never happened. It's annoying how wrong reporters can be. What do you think, Chloe?'

'Reporters are a right bunch of liars,' she replied, stuffing in another cake. 'They write whatever they want or they don't get paid. I wouldn't mind being a news reporter, but I'm not a good writer.'

'What do you think of the report?' I was hoping she'd own up if she was responsible.

'Well, the report said *you* told the story, so someone's pretending to be you and spreading lies. It's Watchett, I bet.'

'No, not this time. He would never be able to look like me anyway! I *know* who made that cow story up,' I said. Tiny sweat droplets formed on Chloe's forehead.

She crammed in another cake and couldn't talk for ages. Perhaps she needed some thinking time.

'Just tell me who it is, Deni, and I'll crush them. I'll rip out their eyes. I'll tear up all their school books . . . I'll . . . OK. . . you know anyway. . . I admit it. I did make up the cow story.' She looked away from me.

'But why did you?'

'For a laugh.'

I expected her to cry.

'When you're finished beating yourself up we can return to normal. I'm not mad with you, Chloe, honest. Especially now you've admitted it.'

She turned back and faced me with large black eyes. 'I thought the extra publicity would help you become that famous adventurer you wanted to be.'

'But I don't need my best friend pretending she's me, making up stories so that I get pestered by reporters who then want more details and I won't have a clue what they're on about.'

'I thought you wouldn't mind.'

'Well I do mind, but I'm thankful it's you in a way.'

'I really am sorry.'

'I'd like you to stop being me and stop making up stories. You're better at being yourself. Now eat that last fairy cake.'

22 My Competition Disaster

Arriving home after school, the stench of a wet bonfire greeted me. I investigated by following my nose to the kitchen and found Dad facing the open oven grill, fanning it with a tea towel trying to clear away the blue smoke billowing into his face. ‘You don’t grill cucumber,’ I said, pushing him aside. I dragged the smoking tray out from under the grill and slung it into the sink. ‘You eat it raw.’

‘I’m simply following a recipe I printed off the internet. It says, “Grill the onions until they are brown and soft.” We didn’t have any onions so I used cucumber.’

‘You can’t just swap food around like that. It’s like saying, “I can’t cut the grass with the lawn mower – I’ll use the car!”’

On the cooker, a frying pan half-full of greasy lumps stank like a pigsty. ‘You’re not frying cornflakes again, are you?’

‘I am.’

‘No, you’re not,’ and I picked up the disgusting fry-up and tipped it into the bin.

‘Shame. Such a good recipe too.’

‘I don’t need all this hassle, Dad. My day’s been hellish; reporters hounded me, Watchett admitted he’d sent me some anonymous texts, and Chloe has been making up stories about me to the newspapers. Now I come back to a house smelling like melting rubber wellingtons about to catch fire! I don’t know which to do first, say hello or call the fire brigade.’

I collapsed into a chair, exhaustion taking over. ‘And how come some reporters knew about our next trip before I did? It’s their job to be seekers of news, but you could have told *me* first, maybe this morning.’

‘Sorry about that, kiddo. I did a little interview for *Film Today* magazine. I told them we were going to the Antarctic to film emperor penguins for *The-Ice-King-Kung-Fu-Cowboy-Computer-Virus-Robbery-Film (with elephants).*’

‘That’s the stupidest film title ever.’ We laughed a bit, which helped to cool the tension.

‘Don’t you think I should have been told first?’ I said, tilting my head to one side and raising my eyebrows. ’I was pestered by reporters outside school today. They knew about the next trip and I didn't. I felt a right hollow head in front of all my schoolmates and teachers. Anyway, I've decided the Antarctic will be my last ever film trip. I've had enough escaping from wild animals and have had more than enough of that publicity rubbish that goes with it. I don't want any more interviews, photographs and questions. If a disaster happens on this next trip I promise I'm *not* going to tell anyone anything, anyhow, anytime, anyplace.'

'If you feel that way, well and good. You can stay behind at Gran's or Lucy's if you prefer.'

'No. I want to go.'

'Well, I'm going to make this trip special – you can bring a friend.'

Clapping and jumping just a little. 'Can it be Chloe? Please?'

'It could be, but we agreed to have a competition.'

'You said *you'd* have a competition. But I'm not going with any old stranger.'

'It won't be a stranger. It's a school competition. You'll know the winner.'

With a finger, he poked the cooling cucumber. It resembled a stiff black sock.

'But my school has its share of odd characters. I'm not going halfway across the world with a creep. What sort of competition do you have in mind?'

He handed me an A3 poster that he'd prepared on his laptop.

Want to go on a lifetime adventure to
the Antarctic?
On DENI TUTTING's next trip?
Then enter this Competition.
Write something about Deni
in 15 words or less.

Send your entry, with your name and class,
to the school office
by next Wednesday.

'That's pretty good – as long as *I'm* the judge.'

'Sorry Deni, but I'm going to judge so it'll be fair and you won't be accused of cheating. I've sorted it with your headteacher. She said I could announce the winner in next Thursday's assembly.'

'Well, we'll look forward to that then,' I said, and marched off to my room to devour half a packet of Hobnobs, two walnut whips, two satsumas and a packet of pig-faced jelly shapes. I had no intention of eating Dad's cucumber bathroom tiles. And Chloe said she'd call over later with some DVDs and a half box of crunchy nut cornflakes. Reach for the spot cream!

I never realised I had so many fans and supporters at school. There were eighty-six entries in the competition and Dad went through each one carefully on Wednesday evening. I admired his focused attention to detail. He sat at the kitchen table for hours sorting the entries into three groups: hopeless, maybe and possible winner.

Chloe came round with a copy of her phrase: *"I've known Deni for ten years and she's my most fantastic and loyal friend."*

'That sounds like a winning entry, Chloe. I'd pick you first if I were judging, but it's all up to his highness. It would be Antarctic-tastic if you could come with us.'

'I'd love to go. Mum and I don't get to go away very often. She says the furthest away we've been is Lowestoft.'

The following morning, Dad and the competition entries came along to our assembly. 'Look at all those kids just waiting for the result,' he said, following the secretary to the stage steps. 'I went to this school when I was a kid,' he told her.

'Deni and Chloe, run along and join your class in the hall,' the secretary ordered.

'Good luck, Dad. I can't wait for the result.' He gave a short wave as we settled into our seats in the front row. Dad stepped onto the stage and sauntered over to the headteacher, Mrs Pothole (nickname 'SpudTank'), who waited by the microphone. On meeting, they shook hands and SpudTank thrust the microphone into Dad's chest. She clomped away, her metal heels pounding and echoing on the wooden boards. Her feet – a human drum kit.

Dad, abandoned in the spotlight, seemed odd up there, out of place. An alien on a new planet. A sausage roll in a sock. A daffodil upside down in a tin of baked beans. (Sorry. Got carried away.)

Before SpudTank reached the exit steps, she stopped as though she had just remembered something, and clomped back to Dad, took back the microphone and said, 'Mr Tutting will, *sometime* today, announce the winner and runners-up of the Deni Tutting 2018 Trip Competition.' Again, she thundered towards the exit.

'Good morning, boys and girls. You're probably not aware but I went to this school in the 1990s. These walls are the same colour now as they were then.' (No response.) 'Thanks for all your thoughtful entries in our Antarctic competition. Every phrase entered was positive. I was not aware just how much Deni is liked and admired.' He raised up the pile of entries and smiled at me. I like to think that he stood there a pleased and proud father. I realised I loved him a lot. (I must remember, while he's in a good mood, to ask for an increase in pocket money.)

'Here's an entry from a boy who's in the early years which impressed me. He wrote: *"Deni is strong like a lion that is VERY VERY strong . . . not as strong as a elephant though."* I liked it a lot but I can't include it because it went over the fifteen-word limit.

'It was a difficult decision but I've selected the winning entry and the lucky winner is coming to the South Pole with us during the Easter break.' He looked down at his cards with the best three entries written on them. 'In third place with: *"I'd love to go on Deni's incredible trip. She's so interesting."* It's Rosalind Butterworth.'

Some feeble clapping arose from different parts of the hall as Rosalind stood up and gave a speedy bow towards the stage. She blushed. Someone giggled and SpudTank peered around the side of the stage and gave the audience one of her *Who did that?* stares – which instantly produced silence.

'In second place with: "*I've known Deni for ten years and she's my most fantastic and loyal friend.*" It's Chloe Clarke. Well done Chloe.'

She stood.

A concentrated burst of vigorous clapping followed. I felt Chloe's disappointment; I shared it too. She glanced at me in disbelief.

She sat.

Her downturned mouth, hidden behind clasped hands, showed a little girl left out of the party. I knew how badly she wanted to win.

That man's let me down again. I believed he liked Chloe but I must be wrong.

He coughed and scratched his head before announcing the winner. (It had better be one of my friends.) 'With an outstanding and thoughtful comment, the winning phrase is . . . *"Deni admits to being a liar, but she doesn't always tell the truth."* That winning entry is by . . . Wendy Charlatan.'

Someone clapped, but no one stood up. Dad repeated, 'The winner is Wendy. Wendy Charlatan. Please stand, Wendy.'

No one stood.

A slightly ruffled SpudTank joined Dad on stage and called out, 'Stand up Wendy. Does anyone know her?'

There was no response for a moment, but then widespread murmuring broke out. It sounded as though the sea had entered the hall. 'Well?' asked the head, putting her hands on her broad hips, pursing her lips and scanning the hall with a *Come out wherever you are* look. Silence returned. Neither cough nor sneeze pierced the air. 'Show yourself Wendy, or the prize will go to second place.' Chloe clapped once.

From the back of the hall, a weak, almost silent voice said, 'I'm Wendy.' And all heads turned to see the shy girl.

Only it wasn't a girl. With a smug grin on his face, Dirk Watchett stood and raised both arms in the air, champion style.

Dad left the hall and I stormed up behind him, grabbed an arm and turned him around. 'You can't allow Watchett to win,' I screeched. 'He cheated.'

'He didn't cheat, Deni, he just used a false name.'

'That *is* cheating, Dad. Some people will do anything to win. Can't you see? False name, false entry!' I stamped my foot.

'I've made my choice and Wendy, I mean Dirk, is coming on our trip.'

I wasn't going to take this decision without a fight. How could my own father allow such a bully and spoilsport to come with us? Chloe made a much better candidate. 'But Watchett said that *I said* I was a liar!'

'Yes, but he also said you don't always tell the truth – which means you are *not* a liar! Clever phrase, yes? That's why I picked it. I wasn't looking to see *who* had written it.

'You know I hate him. He's the last person I'd want on any trip. I'd rather have my appendix out without any painkillers than go on a trip with worm nose. Please, Dad, change your mind.'

'I can't change my mind. The whole school knows the result. I'm sorry you're dissatisfied with the outcome but I don't think we need to discuss it any further.'

I stormed off a short distance, turned and shouted at his back, 'I can't win with you! You never see my point of view. I'm fourteen years old, not two. You should respect my wishes a bit more. And, you're the worst . . . judge ever.'

I gripped my lucky golden charm and chain and yanked it from my neck. It snapped easily. I chucked it like a cricket ball, hitting Dad's right shoulder. 'You can flog that on eBay. I no longer have any need for a useless lucky-ducky-yucky charm. I don't want saving, rescuing or protecting. Furthermore, I refuse to wear any of that smelly army gear on this next trip, so there! (Especially the socks.)

23 The Naughty Spoon

An excited Year 7 boy rang the three-thirty bell on the last day of the spring term. He shook it vigorously. Someone had loosened the handle and the bell came away, flipped to the ceiling and smashed a lamp.

While the ringing still echoed down the long corridor, I rocketed straight up out of my seat and shouted, 'Antarctica – here I come!'

Chloe and I immediately stuffed our school bags with whatever had been sitting on our table and dashed for freedom. 'Walk, you two!' Fiesta called as we passed his classroom in overdrive. We continued to the thick glass doors and the white steps leading down to the road and freedom. I raised my arms in a salute to the sun.

'Don't forget meee!' Watchett shouted, pushing younger kids aside so he could catch us up. He pelted my head with five or six paper snowballs, all of them on target. 'Just practising,' he said, and he blasted a smirk in my direction. My mood graph dived.

I said, 'You can still drop out of the trip, Watchett, if you don't feel up to it. You'd be better off staying at home because it's unbearably cold down south.'

'You'd love it if I dropped out – so Clarke could go instead of me. Well, there's no chance of that happening. Only sickness or injury could keep me from going.'

In a sudden, smooth single move, Chloe and Danny Mulhouse dragged a black wheelie bin liner over Watchett's piggy head and body. Then they pushed him onto the grassy slope beside the steps. He rolled downhill shrieking and tumbled like clothes in a washing machine.

'Just practising, Dirk, you berk,' Danny sang.

We three galloped down the remaining steps and found a slightly dizzy Watchett sitting on the pavement. The rubbish bag lay in shreds around him. He tried standing but wobbled and fell backwards.

'You need a doctor,' said Danny, pushing out his bottom lip to give his medical opinion more power.

'See you at the airport, Watchett,' I said. 'I'll warn security you're coming.'

Yesterday, Danny told me that Watchett fell off the swimming pool's highest board. Fully dressed. Apparently, he ran from a pigeon that had chased him up all the steps to the high board where he walked the plank backwards and plopped below into the deep end. Three swimmers were nearly crushed when he hit the water. I wished I could have witnessed that.

Having Watchett on *my* trip, so close, chatting, laughing and eating with us, was going to be a real pain. What did he want out of this trip? Did he intend to turn it into a disaster? If that was the case, then I'd better make the first move.

Watchett stepped through the airport security metal detector. To his surprise, he set off the alarm. A stern, wide man in a blue uniform, with a pistol at his side, pounced on Watchett as soon as the buzzer buzzed. 'Where are you hiding the machine gun, sonny?'

'What . . . ma . . . ma . . .?'

'Ha, only kidding. But you did set off the alarm.' Watchett suffered a body tremor that began with his lips disco-dancing 1980s style and vibrated all the way down to his cheesy toes. 'Please remove your jacket, belt and snow boots and put all metal objects in this tray.'

Watchett removed the items and into the tray he placed some coins, a bulldog clip, a tiny metal car, a tin of throat lozenges, a pencil sharpener and eight paper clips joined together. 'No wonder you set the alarm off – all that metal! Are you a scrap metal dealer?' Watchett must have felt too scared to answer because he remained silent.

'I'd like you to have a second go through the metal detector, please,' Wide Man said.

Watchett stepped through the detector again. It went off.

Travellers waiting behind me were becoming restless; asking each other what was causing the hold-up. I told them, 'He's like this at school. The doctors can't control his urge to steal metal objects so they lock him up for most of the day. He gets injections every hour and he screams like a toad. This is his first time in public since his parents dumped him at the institute just after his birth. It's all in his risk assessment.'

A woman put her hand to her mouth and muttered, 'The poor angel.'

I continued lying. 'Normally, he's tied up in a special jacket and dumped in the soft room.'

Meanwhile, officer Wide Man scanned Watchett front and back with a hand-held metal detector. 'Raise your arms up, please sonny.'

As his arms went up, Watchett's loose ski-pants went down, showing his pair of *"Happy Feet"* boxer shorts. His face turned the colour of boiled beetroot. The officer searched the fallen ski-pants and found a metal teaspoon in a leg pocket. He held it high for all to see. 'So, we have a spoon smuggler in our midst! Go on, get dressed, sonny, and have a nice flight.'

I'd been checking everything metal that Watchett had put in the tray. No half medal appeared so I could be sure he was not my mystery rescuer.

He gawped at me with blood-shot eyes – rocket launchers ready to fire.

I wonder how that naughty spoon got there!

I smiled a false smile at him as he gathered up his possessions and I mouthed, 'Nice boxers.'

London to Antarctica meant two long flights. The first flew us to the Falkland Islands and I became confused and lost track of meal and sleep times. I thought yesterday was tomorrow, and today was last Tuesday. I woke up for supper, slept past breakfast and had lunch immediately before bedtime! Drowsiness made me pour milk on my toast and spread marmalade on my bacon and I called Dad "Mum" at least twice.

Southern Atlantic icy rain lashed the Falklands, delaying our second flight for two days. A transporter plane, delivering supplies, finally got permission to take off for the South Pole and we travelled in that.

It was cold on the plane. I could see my breath. Thin layers of frost grew on the inside and outside of the windows. But our three actors, film crew and support team, Watchett, Dad and I wore state-of-the-art clothes and ice boots to protect us from the deep-freeze temperatures to come. (I insisted on carrying a parachute for the entire journey and I checked to see if the pilot was that crazy buzzard Lord Abbeville. It wasn't.)

Watchett and I hardly talked. He was still angry with me over the security episode – although he did make some effort to socialise. He followed me around the wide cabin of the transporter plane, waiting to strike. 'I really appreciate being on this trip,' he said. He put out his hand. 'Let's start afresh, shall we Deni?' But my memories of him were mostly unpleasant so I ignored his peace offering, turned away and pretended to read a Spanish magazine. Years of bullying would take a long while to forgive. However, we played noughts and crosses on the frosty windows until our fingers froze (I won).

We landed on a flat runway of snow and ice. Antarctica – the South Pole. Leaving the plane was like entering the coldest freezer imaginable. I could taste the ice in the air. Watchett threw snowballs at the plane and one of the landing crew told him off. A quick stroll across the runway and we arrived at a warm lounge for hot drinks, sausage rolls and cake. I had cake with that and wrapped another bit for later. (So I wouldn't have to break into my secret supply of double chocolate Swiss roll.)

I found a laptop in the games corner of the lounge and printed some holiday suggestions for Watchett. 'I've selected some holidays you might enjoy,' I said, and I handed him the sheet.

Holiday Suggestions for Dirk Watchett

a. Learn yo-yo tricks on Reptile Island, home to the world's deadliest snake.
b. Enjoy a canoe tour of the Quicksand Swamps of Florida, USA (with alligators).
c. Five-day sheep breeding course in Scorpion Valley, India.
d. "Brilliant Holidays for Singles" – a two-week break staying in vampire bat caves, South America, learning; ironing, fish preparation and using a stepladder safely.
e. In Australia. A Survival Skills Course; swim confidently with sharks. Course leader Delgado Rica, (has only one leg and seven fingers).

. . . Could you escape from all these creatures?

A woman in a white overall appeared at the front of the lounge and introduced herself as Dr Denver. 'Ladies and gentlemen, girls and boys, scientists and tourists, welcome to Queen Elizabeth Land research centre. You're in one of the world's most unfriendly surroundings.' Unfriendly it may have been but there were no killer bees, no polar bears, no lions or dingoes, and hopefully no reporters. Just cute, little penguins. This might turn out to be the perfect break.

The doctor continued, 'Your worst enemies are the weather and the temperature. There's to be no going outside unless you are fully geared up and have looked at the TV monitors for the weather forecast. You must tell someone you're going out and you say where you're going. You sign out when you go and in when you get back so we know if you're out or in or in or out.'

Rules, rules, rules. I'm going to have difficulty remembering all those. I noticed Watchett wrote them down in a hard-backed notepad. A white label on the cover read; *DW ANTARCTICA 2018*.

Dr Denver continued, 'Ladies and gentlemen, will you please form a queue at the front of the lounge where you can collect your room key?'

The line of people moved quickly. 'Tom, you and I are sharing a dormitory with six others,' said Dad.

I laughed. 'That's a lot of snoring. Got your earplugs?' I made a snorting noise.

'Miss Tutting, you have a room to yourself,' said the key man. 'East wing, room E5. Blue door.'

We said our goodnights as it was nearly 10 pm. I wheeled my luggage down corridors, across lobbies, up in a lift, round corners and through doors. I had to ask a Chinese man for directions. His English was not clear and I ended up in a radar monitoring room.

E5, when I eventually got there, turned out to be quite luxurious, with a toilet, shower and two bunk beds. I chose top bunk and my luggage chose the bottom.

I unpacked my stuff and found wrapped up in my jeans a small cardboard box attractively tied with a purple ribbon. I opened it to find my half medal on a new gold chain. I felt guilty for having broken my original chain and chucked it at Dad.

In front of the shower room mirror, I clasped the half medal around my neck and whispered, "Thanks Dad. I shall wear it, always – or until my hero shows up."

I grabbed Garlic Breath and climbed the ladder to bed. Under my pillow I had stashed an emergency snack assortment in case of midnight hunger syndrome – a large bag of prawn cocktail crisps, a pack of three walnut whips, a curly whirly and a packet of dark chocolate mini-snowmen (normally for hanging on Christmas trees). On the bottom bunk, for the immediate relief of extreme stomach pangs due to sugar shortage, I'd stashed a jar of Quality Street (minus the triangular ones which I'd already eaten).

My spot cream (night action, full cover-up, with essence of dandelion) stood ready on the bathroom shelf.

I fell asleep thinking about tomorrow – an 'Activity Day.' It's a sort of welcoming start to our visit to the freezing south zzzzzzzzzz.

24 The Winner's Grip

The smell of a proper cooked breakfast reached all the way to my room from the kitchen. My nose dragged me to the canteen where a delicious hot fry-up awaited my stomach. Sausages danced in their tray and the fried eggs gawped up at me gawping down at them. I chose bacon, tomato, hash browns, mushrooms, beans, toast, fried egg, sausage and custard, twice. Then I joined Dad and worm nose at the table.

'I'll be photographing emperor penguins today,' I told Dad and Watchett and I pointed to a large map of Queen Elizabeth Land on the canteen wall. 'D'you see where it says Albert's Gob? Well, I'm heading for that. It's about a mile from here and about a mile from the sea. I'm told that's where I'll find the emperor penguins.'

'That's a strange name for a place, Albert's Gob. Is it a joke?' asked Dad.

'Well, a guy on reception told me it's a place covered in ice mounds that look like Albert's teeth. He lived here a hundred years ago. So they named it Albert's Gob after Albert who had teeth like ice mounds.'

'Stay on the tracks and you should be OK. We'll all be in and around that area so we can keep an eye out for each other. I've been daring and signed up for lessons in snowmobile driving. It's a snow scooter on skis.'

'Sounds fun,' I said, trying out a compass I found in the cloakroom. I faced east. 'What about you, Dirk?' I asked.

Dad spoke up. 'May I suggest we call our competition winner by his preferred name, Tom? Would you be OK with Tom, Tom?'

'Sure, but not Tom-Tom!' He let out a little giggle. 'I prefer Tom, as long as Deni's happy calling me Tom again. It's been a few years since anyone's called me Tom.'

I could have suggested loads of names he *wouldn't* prefer.

'Is Tom OK with you, Deni?' Dad asked. I hesitated in my thinking time. He and Watchett stared at me without blinking, like trout, until I answered.

'I've always liked calling you Tom, so Tom it is.' He appeared to like the sound of his recycled name as he smiled again. I tried keeping upbeat. 'What have you signed up to do today . . . Tom?'

'Snowboarding for me, whoosh! Can't wait.' He imitated a snowboard with a hand that glided across the table knocking over the sugar bowl.

'Looks like you need lessons,' I quipped.

'I'm the best in school on a skateboard,' he boasted. 'But out here, won't the wheels get stuck in the snow?'

'Are you serious, Tom?' I asked. '*Snowboards*, in case you need to know, don't have wheels – they have feet.'

In the few days they'd been together, Dad and Watchett had grown to like each other. They talked and smiled at the same time. They chatted easily about all sorts of things: uses of a drone, bass guitar or acoustic, shave or beard, and how to remove stubborn stains from white T-shirts. I reckoned Dad would have liked a son. I probably could do almost anything Dirk Watchett could do, except put a worm up my nose. He and I were still as far apart as ever.

He'd never been that popular with girls. He quickly switched off, relied on giggling or joking, and was unable to keep a conversation going longer than two sentences. But with other boys or Dad, he coped very well.

Prunella Madigan told me Watchett had been her boyfriend in Year 6, for five and a half days. She was a shy, quiet little mouse then. She said that when they were together she'd fall asleep! That's how interesting he was.

I wished Chloe were here instead of him. She'd have loved to cuddle an emperor (and I didn't mean Napoleon).

'Breakfast over – time to split up,' Watchett announced, stuffing his face with the last half slice of toast. (I'd sprinkled it with a teaspoon of salt.)

We took a moment to check our equipment. Our freezer-proof gear was colour-coded so that we were identifiable from a distance. Dad wore yellow, Watchett red and I wore an orange woollen hat and an orange skisuit. My new goggles were blue. We looked cool.

I carried a flask of water and my digital camera, which dangled on a long strap around my neck.

Watchett pointed out that the TV monitors suggested a return to base by three o'clock. We matched our watches to South Pole time while he threw up salty toast into the waste bucket.

'Look Dad. Tom's too sick to go out today. I think you should send him to bed with a hot water bottle.'

'I'm OK. She put salt on my toast.'

'I don't want my day messed up by you.'

'I have got no intention of messing your day up.'

'Next time I'll use rat poison.'

'You two chill,' said Dad. 'I didn't bring you halfway across the world to argue. We need to get going while there's some good sunlight remaining.'

Having said our goodbyes, I signed out and trundled off along the tourist path that led to Albert's Gob. All tracks in the snow tended to look the same but clear signposts along the way kept me on the right path. A low sun reflected off the snow and ice. I imagined being inside a glass bowl of silvery glitter. 'Welcome Deni, to Tinsel World,' I shouted, knowing I was totally alone.

After an easy stroll of about twenty minutes, I met my first emperor penguin who meandered around like a kid on his first day at school. A second appeared, then more. They were oddly shaped for a bird; a pillow that was white at the front and black at the back. They posed for photos, standing upright like pear-shaped adult humans.

Loud squawking drew me further up a short hill until I became surrounded by chunky, icy blocks resembling Albert's teeth. I stood where I thought Albert's throat might have been. I had a magnificent view of hundreds of emperor penguins huddled together. Keeping a good distance, I approached the colony. The penguins ignored me. Perhaps having no predators meant they were more relaxed around humans. No wonder they were called emperors – they ruled around here for sure.

I put on my extra-large goggles because the sun seemed stronger. As I adjusted them, I thought for a moment that I saw Watchett. Was he spying on me? 'Tom. Are you there?' I called but he didn't show up. It must have been my imagination.

That low sun gave a spooky light, turning the snow in my pictures blue. I fumbled with the camera, searching menus, pressing buttons and arrows hoping to improve the picture quality.

I'd selected "use flash," when loud laughter startled me and I nearly dropped the camera. A laughing emperor, almost my height, stood right in front of me, face-to-face, or should I say beak-to-face? And what a handsome creature – with its bright yellow patches where ears should have been, a black beak with an orange strip and a glossy smooth coat. It repeatedly nodded its head as if to say *yes*, and its breath smelled of tinned sardines.

I raised my camera for a once-in-a-lifetime selfie. I smiled, but I wasn't sure about my penguin friend. I talked to him through my smile, 'Look at the camera.' But sardine breath didn't seem very keen on doing what I wanted. He had a plan of his own.

He stretched open his long beak, grabbed my camera strap and dropped to the ground. I fell and landed on my stomach on ice as hard as concrete. I tugged the strap but the giant bird held it tight.

We lay on the ice entangled but ready for a tug-of-war. 'Let go of my strap, you sardine guzzler,' I said, with no effect.

Paddling his flipper-like wings and kicking his clawed feet, the bird became a speedboat on ice. I felt a sharp pull on the strap, tight around my neck, as together we slid downhill, gaining speed so fast that it became impossible for me to stop. His strength astonished me. He pulled like a powerful car towing a caravan and I was the caravan. Wherever he led, I followed.

What really annoyed me about this penguin – he laughed continuously. It's true! I thought birds chirped or whistled – but not this one.

'Slow down,' I called out, but I was just wasting my breath. Whenever I spoke, he increased his frantic flippering and powerful paddling, sending vast amounts of icy slush straight into my frozen face, frosting up my goggles. I felt my eyebrows thicken as the spray on them froze to solid ice.

I fiddled with the strap, trying to find its buckle, but it was firmly tucked somewhere under my thick collar and I couldn't use my fingers very well because they'd gone numb. Stupid me – I'd removed my gloves back at Albert's Gob before I adjusted the camera. I must have dropped them.

The scraping of my clothes and boots on the ice sounded like a large food mixer going off in my head. I thought I heard words; slow . . . over . . . river, but they made no sense at all.

Seconds later, I realised that the words were spoken by a skier, frantically digging a pair of ski poles firmly into the ice and pushing hard to keep up with us. 'I will cut across . . . try . . . push penguin . . . icy river,' said the skier, but the words were not clear.

I managed to brush the slush from my goggles with my sleeve. The mysterious skier raced ahead, turned sharply in front of us and tried to grab the bird's beak. Penguin must have thought he was under attack from a killer whale, because he ducked, swerved and passed the skier, who lost control of the skis and crashed into a mound of snow.

We continued downhill. Penguin had lost no confidence as a result of the skier's attempt to rescue me.

Who *was* that skier that bravely tried to save me? Didn't the skier say something about an icy river?

Penguin showed no signs of tiredness. His clawed feet peddled like crazy right up to my face. I'd bite them if I could, but they moved too fast.

The laughter seemed louder, wilder, more like a maniac. My stomach ached with all the bouncing and scraping over knife-sharp daggers of ice. I felt there was nothing I could do to release myself from the strap. Did that mean I am to be outwitted by a creature at last; that I had met my match? His grip on my strap was super-tight. To weaken his grip was my only chance of survival.

Some of my previous escapes came back to me just then; a lion on a rope bridge, a sawfish in the middle of the sea, a boxing kangaroo – had I learned anything from defeating them?

Suddenly, a very noisy, yellow blob appeared on my left. I wiped my goggles and saw the yellow – yellow for Dad on his snowmobile. What a relief, rescue at last! I shouted, 'Help me, Dad . . . the strap.' The snowmobile roared. I couldn't tell if he'd heard me over the din of the motor.

He bellowed through his helmet, 'I'll swing over and try to force the penguin to stop.'

'Careful, Dad. This bird's crazy. He'll not give in.'

'You have to stop – you're about half a minute from an icy river.'

"Icy river." The mystery skier mentioned that too. I didn't like any of what I heard.

When the crazy penguin stopped laughing, I guessed something was about to happen. Had Dad's plan worked? I strained my neck and glanced up to see.

Directly in front of us loomed a large rocky lump. Expecting a crash, I covered my head with my arms. Penguin swerved around to the right and I followed, bashing my left leg against the rock as we just scraped past it.

With a quick glance behind me, I saw Dad had steered to the left of the rock and landed his snowmobile in a hole. That was not how it should have been done. After all, hadn't he seen *every* James Bond film? That's where you learn to deal with such unexpected dangers.

The emperor started up his laughing again now he was back on track and heading for the icy river. He must have been thinking, *icy water – my favourite place!* Well, it was far from being *my* favourite place. If he was determined to drag me into the water, I'd freeze in seconds.

We approached the edge of the river at full speed. I quickly sucked in a lungful of air, ready to plunge into the water. However, I noticed a standing figure in red, between the water and us, blocking the way ahead. It was Tom Watchett. Crazy penguin didn't swerve this time but aimed straight at Tom and bashed into his legs. Penguin let go of my camera strap and somersaulted up and over the frozen edge of the riverbank, taking Tom with him. I slid to a stop, rolling into a pile of hard snow and ice.

I heard their splash.

'Tom! Tom!'

I stood up and scanned the scene. The fast flowing river was a menacing sight. There was no sign of the penguin or poor Tom. I called again, but my weak legs gave in and I flopped on to my back and watched my warm breath rise to the sky.

Tom’s snowboard lay where he’d left it, pushed front-end into the snow like a gravestone – his gravestone. On the sloping hillside behind me, his curving snowboard tracks down to the river marked his route on a snowy-white canvas. I called out to the freezing river, ‘My winner, my competition winner, I’m truly sorry to have treated you so meanly. I was such a cow . . . and you . . . who gave your life . . . for . . .’

‘Deni. Is that you?’

Stunned at hearing a voice, I called, ‘Of course it’s me. Where are you?’

‘Look over the edge of the river bank.’

I crawled towards the bank, lay down and peered over the edge. Tom was just below me, perched on an ice ledge, about a metre above the icy water. ‘It’s me, your competition winner!’

‘Tom, you’re alive!’ I blushed, realising he must have heard what I’d just said.

‘That’s very observant of you, Deni. Now can you please haul me up? . . . And you’re not a cow.’

A few days ago, I might have left him there to freeze for a while, but things had changed. He had rescued me from the mad, runaway penguin when others had failed. I felt I owed him a big favour. Or, I owed him my life.

I lay flat and stretched an arm down to him. He grabbed my wrist with both hands. ‘Pull,’ he insisted.

‘I *am* pulling.’

The winner’s grip weakened, losing its strength second by second. My bare hand squeezed but I found lying flat would not allow me to pull Tom up. My arm almost came out of its socket as I heaved and heaved until his hands, then his head, appeared just above the edge of the frozen bank. ‘Guess who?’ he said with a smile. Then, with a jerk and a shrill squawk, his head disappeared back below the bank edge. I was draggednearer the edge too and just managed to stop at the top of the bank by digging my boots into the snow. My arm was at full stretch, yet the winner's grip held tight.

'What the hell's happening, Tom?'

'Your old penguin friend has my left boot in his beak.'

'It can't be the same bird,' I uttered in disbelief. The creature heaved and pulled at Tom's boot, tugging and wriggling, trying to drag us both into the freezing torrent below. It was the same bird – I recognised the haunting laughter.

'I'm losing my footing on this ice ledge, Deni. Can you pull me up again?'

'I'm half over the edge of the bank . . . I've got no way of . . .'

I'd almost lost all hope of saving Tom when I heard Dad shout, 'Hold tight, Tom.' He grabbed my feet and pulled me away from the icy river's edge. Tom followed, with the maniac bird firmly attached to his foot. It flapped its wings, making a clapping sound against its body.

When I felt I was safely away from the river's edge, I felt for the camera around my neck, not sure if it still worked. I approached the penguin as near as I dared, pointed my camera, shouted 'Say sardines,' and clicked.

Blinded by the flash, the penguin squawked, lost his grip and slid back into the river with hardly a splash. The look on its face suggested guilt. This time, I watched him swim out to sea.

We collapsed on to the soft snow.

Tom gave me his gloves. I felt his warmth when I put them on and I felt life slowly drift back into my hands.

'Were you hurt, Tom, when the penguin and I crashed into you?'

‘My snow boots protected me.’ He stretched his legs and knocked the toes of his boots together.

‘Dad and a mystery skier tried to help me on the way down but failed. I’m so grateful you were there to stop me plunging into the river. ’

Tom pulled his hood over his head and stuffed his bare hands into his pockets. ‘I noticed from the top of the hill that you were in trouble. I took a shortcut to beat you to the water’s edge.’

‘If not for you Tom, I’d be an ice mummy by now and that mad penguin would be riding me like a surfboard above the waves and out to sea.’

There was a whoosh of snow as our mystery skier arrived. Tom stood. ‘Who are you, if I may ask?’ he said.

‘Deni knows me,’ the skier replied, pulling off her hat and ski mask.

‘Queen Kaarma!’ I shouted. Dad smiled.

‘When I heard you were going to Antarctica I arranged for my private jet to bring me here. I find it far more comfortable and faster than travelling by donkey.’

I introduced Tom to Queen Kaarma.

‘And to you, Dad, for pulling us to safety, I give a loving, Tutting cuddle.’ I squeezed him tightly.

‘Deni, you have three rescuers here,’ he said. ‘One of us *is* your hero. Guess.’

‘I thought you said we weren’t going to play guessing games ever again.’

‘This isn’t the Birthday Box, Deni.’

‘It’s still guessing,’ I pouted.

‘I’ll never again ask you to guess.’

‘Well, for a start, it isn’t you, Dad. You drove your snowmobile down a hole.’

‘But I did pull you clear of the river. That counts.’

‘True. I’ll bear that in mind.’

Smiling at Queen Kaarma, I said, 'It could be you, Your Majesty, because in the hotel in Australia, I saw Dad give you a small box – which could have contained the other half of my medal.'

'You're quite a detective, aren't you Deni? I'm afraid there was no medal in that box, only the key to Tonsil's prison. I've carried it for good luck ever since.' She took the object from inside her jacket and held it up. 'This reminds me how fortunate I am to have met your father who rescued me from hell.' The key glistened. 'I had it gold-plated. But, I'm sorry to say, Deni, I am not your matching half medal.'

I turned to Tom. 'I can hardly believe that I'm here, all thanks to you, Tom. If you hadn't turned up and forced that penguin into the river, I'd be a human ice lolly bobbing along in international waters with crabs and sardines nibbling at my flesh.

He looked at me, not with his normal gawp, but I guessed with feeling and with tenderness. 'You rescued me too, Deni. I'll never doubt you again.'

From around his neck he pulled and tugged on a golden chain until his half of the talisman appeared. I fitted my half to his and Dad said, 'A perfect match.' A zap of electricity ran up my arm from my fingers holding the medal.

I smiled my first proper smile in ages.

'I declare Tom to be my rescuing hero – and, do you know what? I think I do believe in luck and it was the talisman that brought it.' Dad and Queen Kaarma clapped. I felt as though I had passed a difficult exam.

A sudden blast of colder air brushed snow dust into our faces. 'Time to be heading back,' Dad said.

Queen Kaarma climbed on to the snowmobile behind Dad, placing her skis over her shoulder. I waved.

'Tom and I will walk back. See you later.'

The motor started and the snowmobile headed off up the hill leaving a cloud of icy dust that danced in the light of the low sun. Tom and I trod slowly through knee-deep snow, following the track he'd made earlier on his way down.

No sadness was felt in leaving the ice river. There lingered inside me a glow of hope. Hope for less hassle. I even felt sorry for the crazy penguin. No doubt he could take care of himself - an excellent swimmer. I believed he would find the way back to his colony.

I looked at my new . . . friend, unsure if *friend* was the right term to use.

'Tom. I don't want any more pestering from you. I want a future without hurtful words.'

'Agreed. And I'm glad you're calling me by my true name.'

'And I'm glad that you're glad . . . Wendy!'

I smiled and he laughed, and it sounded like a real laugh, not like a put-down sneer.

'And promise you'll be especially respectful towards Chloe when we get home.'

'Always.'

'And you and I will each treat the other as we would want to be treated ourselves.'

'Big time.'

'Life's going to be vastly improved for us and everyone around us.'

'Guaranteed.'

'And Tom, neither I nor you will tell anyone about our penguin adventure. It will be the best-kept secret forever. Is that agreeable?'

'You betcha.'

Dad and Queen Kaarma reappeared on the snowmobile and drove around us in a series of wide circles. From the back seat, her majesty called out, 'New friends are hard to find!'

'Don't encourage them,' Dad added, half turning his head towards the Queen.

Meanwhile, pure clouds of powdery snow rose up from the snowmobile's tracks to form a foggy, white dome above both of us. We became a wintery scene locked inside a giant snow globe. I felt protected – even more so now that Tom had agreed to behave himself.

Through the mist of snow, I took one last glimpse of the long slope we had whizzed down so dangerously.

That tangle of footprints and ski tracks, fear and courage, began to disappear as the sun lowered. What footprints would we make in our futures? What tracks would we leave behind in our stories? Who can tell?

However, I can be sure of one thing – that thick flakes of freezing snow would soon fall and cover up those tracks, leaving our adventure not seen and not told.

Epilogue

'Here is the latest news from the Australian outback Radio Dustbowl, brought to you by Heather McNulty.

'A man, who was locked inside his campervan for four days, lived entirely on fish food and dog food. His wife will be taking him for a walk later, if he's a good boy.

'In Gulamontan, an 89-year-old grandmother ate three cockroaches thinking they were dates left over from Christmas. "They tasted like belts," she said.

'But first, news of a mad kangaroo running in a zigzag manner along the beach road this morning precisely at seven o'clock. Witnesses said it was hitting its pouch, frothing at the mouth and sounding like an alarm clock. Police have advised members of the public not to approach the creature after it robbed a petrol station and got away with 13 bags of extra-chilli chips and a bottle of barbecue lighter fluid.

'You've been listening to Radio Dustbowl. I'm Heather McNulty. Have a g'day.'

Meet the Author

Rick has told humorous stories for many years, as a child, as a teacher and as a parent. He has observed children engaging with stories, especially those containing humour. 'There is often a serious side to events too. Life isn't just full of funny bits.'

He is the author of a guidebook to unusual buildings and curiosities in the east of England and recently had a short story published in an Essex anthology.

The Winner's Grip is Rick's first novel. 'I hope it entertains. Perhaps I can begin my next novel now.'

Printed in Poland
by Amazon Fulfillment
Poland Sp. z o.o., Wrocław